CHRISTMAS CONFUSION
CHRISTINA SINISI

CHRISTMAS CONFUSION by Christina Sinisi

ANAIAH SEASONAL
An imprint of ANAIAH PRESS, LLC.
7780 49th ST N. #129
Pinellas Park, FL 33781

This book is a work of fiction. All characters, places, names, and events are either a product of the author's imagination or are used fictitiously. Any likeness to any events, locations, or persons, alive or otherwise, is entirely coincidental.

The Christmas Confusion copyright © 2019 Christina Sinisi

All rights reserved, including the right to reproduce this book or portions thereof in any form. For inquiries and information, address Anaiah Press, LLC., 7780 49th ST N. #129 Pinellas Park, Florida, 33781

First Anaiah Seasonal print edition November 2019

Edited by Kara Leigh Miller
Book Design by Anaiah Press
Cover Design by Laura Heritage

To Kyle, You're Right Where I Belong.

ACKNOWLEDGEMENTS

I've been writing my whole life, so there have been many who have helped me along the way. In my writing life, Eloisa James has been a mentor and friend. She's read my work, shared it with others, and encouraged me like only she can. Closer to home, Dianne Miley and Kieran Kramer, have critiqued and suggested and helped me eat my way around the LowCountry. To paraphrase, the price of good friends is beyond rubies.

For this particular story, I am indebted to Christina Clark and her husband Jason Chapman, police officers for Colleton County, South Carolina. I know I have so much to learn about what you do, but thank you for getting me this far. I also appreciate Nick Long, ex-Marine (are you ever ex?) for insight into the war in the Middle East.

Thank you very much to the Anaiah Press team, Kara Miller and Melinda Dozier and more--you worked so hard to make this book the best it could be!

Thank you to my husband, Kyle, children, Scott and Lindsey, my mama, Linda, and sisters, Carol and Sherry, for always loving and supporting me.

Finally, thank you, Jesus, for everything.

CHAPTER 1

SOMEONE HAD STOLEN HER BLACK heels. That was the only explanation. Tiffany Marano had checked her bedroom closet—where they belonged. That's where she'd left them. Now, she was working her way through the cavernous hall closet, which seemed to contain half the items she'd been missing. But not her shoes. If this closet didn't produce results, then she'd have to bend down in this skirt and search under the couch, a very bad idea.

The Santa ornament wearing beach shorts and flip-flops randomly started singing about an island Christmas. She groaned. The volume seemed permanently set on "annoy the neighbors"—the last thing she needed was for them to complain about the noise again.

"I don't have time for this." Tiffany raced down the hallway and grabbed Santa off her miniature Christmas tree. She slid across the bare pine floor in her stocking-clad feet and flailed her arms. By some small miracle, she grabbed a wall to stop her forward progress.

After a deep breath of relief—and a few more seconds of auditory torture by a Christmas recording—Tiffany crept down the hall, trying to avoid another near wipeout. She stepped on her niece, Haley's, hair barrette. "Ouch, ouch." She whisper-shouted, hopping like a crazy woman. *Thunk.* Her forehead made contact with the open guest-bedroom door. She closed her eyes against the pain. For a few minutes, she gripped the doorframe with one hand and her head with the other. Santa reached the chorus.

Haley stood at the end of the hall, eyes wide. "Aunt Tiffy, are you okay?"

Tiffany nodded. She clapped a hand over Santa's tiny mouth. She glanced at her niece, who was also without shoes, as if the lack was contagious. "Haley, I thought you were dressed. If we don't hurry, we're going to be late for church."

"Yes, ma'am." The girl giggled and ran down the hall, skating in her socks on purpose.

Tiffany tried not to laugh, because moving hurt her head. She stuffed the Santa in her pocket, walked into the bathroom, and switched on the lights. She contemplated the red mark on her forehead in the mirror. "Great," she whispered. "That's going to bruise."

Not good. In less than an hour, if she made it out of this apartment alive, she would need all the energy she could get to teach an energetic bunch of preschoolers about Jesus. Every parent would see the evidence of her klutziness one more time. "Oh well." She leaned forward so her dirty-blond bangs covered the angry welt. "I am who I am."

She shoved Santa in the linen closet between two monogrammed towels and found her shoes by the tub.

Half an hour later, she held Haley's hand and stumbled into the church fellowship hall. The low-slung brick building was nestled against a busy road in Summer Creek, South Carolina, and the late-autumn sun showered pale light on the white roof. It was cold enough they were both wearing long sleeves and light jackets, but that was more than enough. Die-hard leaves held on to the ornamental pear and rustled as they hurried past. Despite insulting the speed limit on the way, Tiffany was now late.

"Tiffany, sweetheart." Mrs. Melanie, the Sunday school director, rushed toward her before she even reached the coffee line. There should be a law against speaking to someone before she'd had a chance to pour her coffee and choose between breakfast casserole and a doughnut.

"Good morning, Mrs. Melanie," Haley chirped. "We're running late. We overslept."

"Did you now?" Mrs. Melanie's glasses fell down her nose, and she pushed them back with her ever-present clipboard. "Well, that's all right, sweetheart. You're here now, and that's all that matters."

Haley beamed, and her missing-one-tooth smile lit up the big room. "Yes, ma'am." Haley danced from one foot to the other. "And there are doughnuts. Can I have a doughnut, Aunt Tiffany?"

Tiffany gave an answering smile. Her niece's joy was contagious and almost had her giving in to temptation herself. "Yes, you may, but I can't. I've eaten like a pig this week, and Christmas is coming."

"And yet you stay so skinny." Mrs. Melanie handed Haley a napkin. "So, Tiffany, you might wonder why I grabbed you as soon as you came in. I just got a text from Mr. Billy, and he can't teach the young adults this week. He was up all night with some stomach bug. I know you expected to teach the little ones, but I can get one of the high schoolers to do that. Lauren already said she would."

Tiffany had to still be asleep, and this was the start of the nightmare where she showed up to class in her ducky pajamas, completely unprepared for the final exam. "I'm sorry. What?"

Mrs. Melanie waved the clipboard like a red flag. "I know it's short notice, but they're just reading *The Relationships Guide*. It's a discussion group, and you read the book with us in women's book club last year."

The special chocolate-chip pancakes she'd reheated for Haley's breakfast churned in Tiffany's stomach. Could the woman hear herself talk? They'd read the book last year. There was no way Tiffany remembered the material well enough to lead a discussion.

"I'd do it myself, but I promised I'd read the Scripture in second service." The church offered a service at the same time as Sunday school, which sometimes caused conflicts, like now. "Will you do it?"

Tiffany wasn't perfect. Church was a place for imperfect people. One of Tiffany's imperfections, one she'd given up on ever curing, was her inability to say no. "Um, sure. Just let me—"

"Here's the teacher's edition of the book." Mrs. Melanie interrupted before Tiffany could finish her thought, which was good because rational thought had clearly left her brain. "I'll just take Haley to her classroom so you can glance through it."

If Tiffany tackled the Sunday school director in the middle of the fellowship hall, would a judge be merciful, or would there be additional years added to the sentence? Resigning herself to the inevitable, Tiffany smiled and took the book. "Thank you. You be good in class, Haley bug."

"You, too." Haley's powdered-sugar-coated face gleamed. "Bye, Aunt Tiffy."

"Bye." She hugged her niece and thanked the Lord for white blouses. "I'll come get you from your class. You wait for me."

The little girl waved with her free hand, and Tiffany watched her go. An elderly man coughed behind her, and she got busy putting hazelnut creamer in her coffee. A quick swirl with a stir stick, and she got out of his way. Book tucked under her arm, she headed for an empty table at the back of the fellowship hall. The fellowship hall held one large room for the church's social events with classrooms around the sides of the room. It wasn't the best arrangement for acoustics and space for the different age groups, but the family feeling of the congregation made up for the few negatives. Tiffany loved it here.

She took a long sip of her too-hot coffee and steeled herself.

There was a lesson plan. The book had been written in short, two-page lessons with Scripture on one side and questions on the other, and this week's lesson was about the lack of constancy in humankind. Tiffany could write a book on this chapter. She gulped her much-needed caffeine fix and headed to the young adults' classroom.

A man she didn't recognize from behind opened the door before she got there and, gentleman that he was, stepped aside to let her enter first. Her sleep-befuddled mind registered thick shoulders, a broad back, and brown curls that tipped over his blue button-down collar. Other than that, she murmured a quiet, "Thank you," and focused on the rest of the class. The man behind her might be a stranger, but the rest of the class was very familiar to her.

"Hi, Tiffany," her friend Valerie said from the far side of the circle of chairs. "What brings you to our neck of the woods? The little ones too tame for you?"

Tiffany's spirits lifted at the sight of the petite, slightly curvy twentysomething girl. They'd met in middle school, and Valerie had been the one to stick by her through her misfortunate middle-school hairstyles and the heartbreaks of high school. Valerie made her laugh, and if she was in this class, all would be well. "Mrs. Melanie asked me to sit in for Mr. Billy."

Valerie's husband, Travis, looked up from his notebook with concern in his bespectacled eyes. "Is he all right?"

Tiffany lost the smile that had started. "Actually, Mrs. Melanie said he has a stomach bug. So, let's add him to our prayers. Don't let me forget." She took the unoccupied seat on Valerie's left and murmured greetings to the others in the room before shifting in her chair and paying attention to the stranger in their midst. *Sweet baby Jesus.*

He wasn't a stranger. At least, she'd known him better than anyone else on the planet a lifetime and seven years ago. Nick Walsh had been her senior prom date. He'd brought her flowers and literal fruit in a basket when she'd had the car accident that totaled her precious first car. He'd sat in the dining room and talked to her mom for hours, even after everyone else had long left her graduation party and he'd been given every hint that it was time for him to go home.

Then, he had enlisted in the Marines and disappeared from her life.

Long-scarred-over pain washed over her like rain, and she wanted to disappear from this classroom—maybe from her hometown.

CHAPTER 2

"TIFFANY." NICK ACKNOWLEDGED HER WITH a lift of that cleft chin, which caused a domino effect of his thick hair falling into his brown, almost night-black, eyes. "Good to see you."

"Good to see you, too," she answered reflexively because her brain went on autopilot. The rest of her body felt as if she'd been shot with Novocain, numb but very much able to feel the heavy pressure and prodding of buried memories. Her automatic response was certainly better than the insults and accusations that started flying around in her brain like mutated monkeys. He was a liar and a coward and no better than the father who had left him behind when he was just a kid.

"Have you been coming to Grace for long? I hadn't seen you." Her voice faded, and she gave a small laugh. "Of course, I'm usually trying to keep the little ones corralled before most people arrive."

He gave her a level gaze, absent the vacant smile she wore like armor. "No, this is my first week. I hope that's okay, starting in the middle of the book like this."

"It's absolutely okay," Mr. Kinney, a church elder with a young soul, said. "We've really only started. In some other book, chapter eight might be pretty far along, but these lessons are so short we usually cover two a week."

Liz Breslin stood and held out a hand to the newcomer. The youngest of the group, she'd just turned twenty this spring, and Tiffany knew because she'd gone to the girl's celebration lunch. Liz had this vibrant way about her, cheeks always rosy, long black hair always bouncing in a waist-long braid.

"Welcome to Grace Church. So good to have another young person." The rosy cheeks got rosier. "I mean, not that there aren't young people already. And not that older people aren't wonderful." Liz dropped her hand before Nick could even take it and took her seat. "I'm sitting down now before I can do any more damage."

Where Nick had stared Tiffany down with the solemnity of a judge, Liz's awkwardness had him grinning. He got up and shook the girl's hand. "Thank you for the welcome. And you are?"

"Liz." Her voice was breathless. Nick had that effect on women—knocked the intelligence right out of them. "I'm Liz Breslin."

"Well, I'm Nick Walsh." He took his seat. "I used to attend Grace in high school. Then, I signed up with Uncle Sam, and the rest is history."

A quick murmur went around the room. The last of their little group, Tyler Burgess, sat straighter in his chair. Tyler was one of those men who attended rarely and sat in the back of the sanctuary. Tiffany was surprised to see him in this class. "Thank you for your service," he said in a deep, serious voice.

Nick nodded. "So," he said, shifting the attention back to Tiffany, "I didn't know I needed to bring a book. Are there extras?"

Tiffany inhaled. This wasn't her classroom, and his guess was as good as hers. She looked to Valerie for a lifeline. Her friend jumped up and opened a cabinet door. "Here. You can use Anthony's. He's out with the flu."

"Seems like a lot of that's going around." Tiffany tried to let her friend know how much she appreciated the help with a small smile. She pulled out the binder she brought with her to church every Sunday. One thing she felt comfortable doing, no matter the age of her students, was taking prayer requests. "Let me start a joys-and-concerns list."

The regulars started right in with the good and bad things going on in their lives. Tiffany wrote them down and added the joy of her job and getting to babysit her niece. She omitted the exhaustion she'd been feeling this second year of teaching. Last year, she'd had an overwhelming sense of not knowing what she was doing after finishing her undergraduate and master's degrees back to back. Student teaching had been one thing. Being alone in one's own classroom was a different beast. She'd gotten past that first year only to face a group of children that would make experienced teachers weep.

She might have shared her weakness with the parishioners she knew so well, but she'd be hung out to dry before she admitted her misgivings in front of the man who had planted some of those self-doubts so long ago.

Nick had been rather quiet himself. She asked for any last-minute additions. "If y'all don't mind," he said, his voice soft, "please pray for me and my daughter. We just moved back to town, and the transition is going to be—has already been—tough."

His daughter. Tiffany inhaled heated air that chilled on the way down. He wore a wedding ring— she hadn't checked before—and he had a daughter.

She simply wrote his name down, but inside, the heartbreak made her want to cry. "Your daughter's name?" She looked in his general direction, not allowing herself to meet his eyes. She could not be attracted to another woman's husband, even if she had been in love with the man years before.

"Elloree."

A hot wave of hurt swept over her. Elloree was the name of a town on the way to Columbia, the state capital. At the end of their senior year, mere weeks before he got in his truck and drove out of her life, they'd gone to the zoo in the city an hour and a half away. They skipped a day of school—senior skip day—and explored all by themselves, away from the prying eyes of their parents and the teasing of their friends. It was better than prom and homecoming all wrapped in one. On the drive back, she said how much she liked the name for a little girl someday.

"We thought she was going to be a boy." He stared at her, his face one big blank. "It was the first name that came to me when she was born and I found out she was a girl. I guess technology can be wrong sometimes."

"Oh, okay. Thank you," she managed to say and wrote down the name. This was a living nightmare, and her quota for surprises was full. She inhaled slowly. "If you will all bow your heads with me."

Somehow, she found the words. She praised the Lord and thanked Him for allowing them to come to Him in prayer. Then, she cheated and read from her list of joys and concerns. The list hadn't been long, but she knew better than to trust her memory. There were loved ones who had cancer, and Liz would be taking final exams next week. She finished with a request for the care of Nick and his daughter. She said "Amen" and listened to the echoing *amen*s around the room, allowing the peace to restore her calm to some degree.

She opened her eyes and flipped pages to find chapter eight. "So, how do you do this?" She rested a finger on the top of the page. "Do you read the text and then answer these questions?"

Valerie squeezed her arm. "You do you, sugar. We'll follow along."

Tiffany wanted to protest but accidentally met Nick's steady gaze. Her cheeks heated. "Okay. Let's read a few paragraphs at a time. I like breaking it down that way."

They were only a few paragraphs in when Nick coughed.

"What?" Tiffany glanced up from the book, startled. "Are you okay?"

"Yes. Sorry about that." He didn't look apologetic. Instead, if she wasn't at church, she'd say the man had a mocking sneer on that handsome face.

"Well." Tiffany hesitated and then took the plunge. She might not want to hear what he had to say, but the instructions did say to discuss. "If you have something to say, that is kind of the point."

"Well." He mimicked, but she let the insult slide, for now. He leaned forward, elbows on his thighs. "It's been my experience that women tend to have a lot more of those ups and downs, but the author acts like we're all the same."

Valerie squared her small shoulders. "Are you saying women are less constant than men? I'd challenge that assumption, given the number of men who cheat, present company excluded, of course." She dimpled a smile at her husband, and he tilted his chin in acknowledgment.

Nick crossed his arms, muscles bulging, forming a barricade between him and the rest of the group. "You can leave a relationship without cheating. I'm just saying women are a lot more likely to get upset and then turn around and act like everything should be okay."

Tiffany was quiet, but he never stopped staring at her as if she were the reason he felt this way. Which would be ridiculous since he was the one who'd said one thing and done another.

"Well, since I'm a man, I can argue the other side with impunity," Mr. Kinney said. "I don't think either sex has a corner on inconstancy. We just react differently. Some people face their downs, and others run."

She pictured herself yelling "So, there," but she sat meekly in her chair. For now, given that they were in church, she'd behave. But later? She made no promises.

"Can I read the next paragraph?" Tyler spoke for the first time since his non-informative introduction.

Tiffany realized she and Nick hadn't taken their eyes off each other. Uncomfortable, she switched her attention to Tyler, who riffled the pages of his book as if even mild conflict made him nervous. "Sure."

Tyler read the rather long paragraph about the purpose of the downs in our lives. The text hammered the point that God allows humans to go through the tough times so they'll rely on Him and that the hard times might be more important than the good times. When he finished, he leaned back in his chair, self-satisfied. "So, if women experience more of those down times, it could explain why more women attend church."

Nick gave the other man a quick salute. "Point scored, especially since I haven't attended in years. I guess I was focusing on the other person's sin and not my own."

"We all do that," Tiffany said in a softer tone. She wanted to be a member of a welcoming church and hoped it didn't come off as artificial, given her very mixed feelings about this particular newcomer's presence.

Nick nodded in her direction, but he never smiled at her. He looked as if there was as much going on behind the scenes with him as there was with her. "Okay. I'll read the next paragraph, then?" He didn't wait for her approval, just barreled through. After a very long paragraph that applied the Scripture to sticking it out in relationships, particularly marriages, his eyebrows lifted. "The next one's real short. Shall I?"

"Yes, please."

He finished and then flipped back through the pages. "Who wrote this? They seem to think they've got this relationship thing all figured out."

The class burst out in laughter, and Nick ducked his head. "Well?"

"Our pastor." Tiffany struggled to speak over the fading roar. "He really is a marriage counselor on the side."

"Ah." Understanding dawned in those dark chocolate eyes. "Don't tell him I said that, okay?" He leaned back, a smirk on his face. "Still think women are less constant."

It was a challenge, and it didn't make sense.

She flipped the page, trying to convince herself that she could be unflappable if she put her mind to it. "Shall we go on to the next lesson?"

"Um." Mr. Kinney shifted on the metal folding chair. "Maybe we should wait on that one."

Another of Tiffany's flaws that she swore she'd cure someday was her inability to switch gears. She'd been tossed into this classroom, and all she knew to do was to read the book and discuss it. She knew Mr. Kinney was wise and she should take his advice, but—oh, no—she'd started down this path, and onward ho.

Thus, she spent the next half hour talking about the temptation of sex and attacks on one's faith. If she'd been more uncomfortable in her life, she didn't know it. She and Nick hadn't gotten that far, all those years ago, but they'd ventured too close. One of their problems had been the stereotypical arguments where the boy wanted more than the girl wanted to give.

Funny—her bitterness had submerged the problems they had before his abrupt departure from her life. All she'd remembered was the laughter and the fire and then the gone.

When they finished the second lesson, Tiffany, happy that it was over, asked Mr. Kinney to close them out with prayer.

He pushed back his chair to stand. They formed a circle, and Tiffany sent up a pre-prayer of gratitude that Liz and Tyler were the ones standing next to Nick and loosely holding his hands.

Mr. Kinney bowed his head. "Dear Lord, thank You for this opportunity to come learn about You and Your plans for our relationships with each other. Please be with each of these young people as they go through the upcoming week, and keep us all safe. In Jesus's name, amen." They opened their eyes, and Mr. Kinney held out a hand. "Thank you, Miss Tiffany. I know this had to be hard to do last minute like this."

Relief made her feel giddy. "You're welcome, and really, you all didn't need me."

Valerie gave her a quick hug. "Maybe we didn't need you, but we were glad to have you. And you, too, Nick. It's been a long time since we've seen you."

Tiffany blinked. She'd been so overwhelmed by her own memories that she'd forgotten she wasn't the only one in the room who knew Nick. Valerie had been her best friend for years, and they'd all been part of the youth group.

Nick found himself wrapped in one of Valerie's signature hugs. The girl made up for her lack of height with extreme gusto. The six-foot-something man—and he'd grown since she'd last seen him—patted her friend's back as if she were a child. "Good to see you, too, Valerie."

She released him and hurried to grab her purse. Travis shook his head at his wife in amusement. "Hey, she might be a fireball, but she's my fireball."

"Good to see you, Travis." Nick slapped the other man's arm.

Tiffany had stood there gawking while everyone but the two of them vacated the room. Now, she felt like an idiot for not running while she could. "Well, I need to go pick up Haley."

Nick once again held the door for her. "So, how are you, Tiffany?"

His voice must have dropped an octave because the depth sent shivers down her spine. He was married. The bitterness in his voice while he accused women of being the more inconstant sex might not have been aimed at her. He had also asked for prayers for himself and his daughter as if his wife wasn't part of the picture.

He wore the ring.

Confusion almost overwhelmed her. "I'm fine," she finally said.

The polite follow-up would have been to ask after his health, as well, but there were so many other questions piling up in her head that she ended up saying nothing. Plus, the distance between the young adults' classroom and the preschoolers' was only a matter of a few steps.

"Daddy!" A little girl with a pink polka-dot bow perched crookedly on top of a mass of brown curls escaped the high-school-aged warden who had been blocking the door with her body. There was no mistaking the genetic connection between the little girl with the big sunflower eyes and the man who scooped her up in his arms.

When the dam burst and let loose one little fishy, the others followed in a flood. Haley had her arms wrapped around Tiffany's knees before she could process the pain that sliced through her at watching Nick hold another woman's child. He'd been out of her life for years, so why did she feel like this? "Hey, Haley." She rubbed her niece's head. "What'd you learn today, bugaboo?"

"I learned about Jesus, just like always." Haley sounded like the lesson was old hat, when, truth be told, the little girl came to church only when Aunt Tiffany brought her. She was super intelligent, though, and often drove her mother over the edge with all her questions.

Tiffany looked at Lauren, her substitute teacher. "How was she?"

"She was great." The girl spoke with enthusiasm, which wasn't a good indicator of the child's behavior. Lauren tended to ooze awesome.

"Did you behave, Elloree girl?" Nick looked at his daughter sternly as if he understood the high-school-aged teacher wasn't going to say a bad word about anybody.

"Yes, sir." The daughter sounded as if she were saluting a superior officer. "Best behavior, Daddy."

Nick glanced in Tiffany's direction, and pride surged through her that she had progressed to the "meeting his eyes as if there wasn't a past a mile wide between them" stage. "She's a lovely little girl."

For a heartbeat, Tiffany had no idea what he was talking about. Then, realization dawned. "Oh, Haley isn't—"

Before she could finish the thought, Elloree grabbed her daddy's face between her two small hands. "I have to go to the potty, Daddy. And I mean now."

"All righty, then." The big man's chiseled cheekbones flushed a bright red, and it was the best sight Tiffany had seen all day. "Well, I guess we'll see you next week."

She deflated, shoulders dropping. Church was her sanctuary, and she didn't know whether she could face a lifetime of seeing him in another pew with the absent wife who would certainly arrive at some point. "Yes, have a good week. Good to meet you, Elloree."

"Daddy." Her whine could destroy a chalkboard.

"Bye." He grimaced and started to move past her. When he drew even, though, he frowned. His free hand rose as if by its own accord, and he moved her bangs to the side. "Ah, Tiffany, what'd you do?"

"Long story," she answered, even though her brain synapses had been short-circuited by the electricity his touch sparked in every cell of her body.

"Same old Tiff." He gave a crooked, side grin. "Watch out for your mama, Haley." He looked down at the little girl with a wink and was gone.

"Why'd he want me to watch out for my mama?" Haley let go of Tiffany's knees and peered up with those so-bright blue eyes. Every member of their family had those eyes. "Is something wrong?"

Tiffany shook her head and squatted to look her niece in the eye. "No, nothing's wrong. He just thought I was your mama since I'm here with you. Next time, I'll be sure to make it clear I'm your aunt."

"Oh." Haley squinted. "I'm hungry."

Tiffany stood and captured the little girl's hand. "Good thing it's lunchtime, then. What do you want to eat?"

"Cheese pizza!"

"Can't. We don't have time to order. Your mom will be picking you up before you know it." She swung their arms in a big arc to take the bite out of her no. "I'll make us lunch at home. How about bugs on a rug?"

They walked and talked, Tiffany trying to focus on the precious child at her side.

Her body still reeled from Nick's touch. After all these years, he could take her breath away. He'd also been the only one to notice the injury and remind her of just how flawed she was.

At the same time, he was the only one to notice because he had always been the only one to see the real her.

CHAPTER 3

HALEY CHATTERED NONSTOP THROUGH LUNCH. They'd arrived at Tiffany's apartment, changed out of their Sunday best, and scrounged for something that could be prepared fast. Bugs on a rug—peanut butter and celery with raisins randomly stuck in—made a fun snack while Tiffany heated soup and grilled cheese.

The little girl's conversation didn't exactly demand an adult's full attention, so Tiffany's mind wandered where it would, and it was back on every gesture Nick had made throughout their little-over-an-hour encounter this morning. They hadn't seen each other in over seven years. A lot could happen in seven years.

He was married and had a child. Yet he'd touched her with the same old affection as if nothing had changed.

"Is it time for me to go home?" Haley's hand on her arm interrupted her long black train of thought. "I'm sleepy, and I miss Jimbo."

Jimbo was her Yorkshire terrier puppy. Emma, Tiffany's youngest sister, spoiled her little girl, but since there was no daddy in the picture, there was no one to stop the spoiling. Not that adopting a puppy was a bad thing, if Emma could afford it, but she couldn't. Emma worked as an office manager during the week and as a waitress on the weekends. If Tiffany didn't babysit Haley, the little girl would never have seen the inside of a church. As it was, Emma often kept her home on those Sunday mornings when her shift started later in the day.

Tiffany was fighting a battle for her niece's character and soul.

"Don't get me wrong," the four-year-old child said with all the seriousness of a mature adult. "I love being with you, and I love Jesus, but I need a nap."

It was part of their deal that Tiffany brought Emma a sleepy little girl so she could get some rest after working so much. Tiffany leaned over and squeezed the girl tight, inhaling the sweet child smell. "I love being with you, and I love Jesus, too. Let me text your mom and see if she's home yet."

"Okay." Haley went back to driving her celery stick around her plate like a toy car.

Tiffany grabbed her empty plate and glass and stashed them in the sink. Her phone sat on the kitchen shelf as far away from the dishwater and potential destruction as possible yet still within eyesight so she wouldn't end up spending hours trying to find it.

CHRISTMAS CONFUSION

Hey, are you ready for Haley? She's ready to come home. I got her all nice and tired just for you. You're welcome.

She hit send and put the phone back in its designated spot. It was early, and her sister probably wouldn't be back home until the lunch crowd dissipated. Still, Tiffany was in the habit of making her niece feel safe when she stayed over, and texting her mother when she asked was part of the deal.

"Tell you what, Haley bug." She sneaked the unfinished food away to be trashed. "Let's color a picture for your mom while we wait for her answer."

"Okay." Haley jumped up and plopped down on the couch. From experience, the girl knew the coloring books and crayons were stashed under the coffee table. Tiffany washed the dishes by hand. If she waited for enough to accumulate to fill the dishwasher, she'd be waiting for days.

A quick check of her phone revealed no answer. Haley's face-sized yawn was catching, and Tiffany covered her face with both hands. "Hey, why don't you come to my room and we'll snuggle? Your mom hasn't answered yet."

"She's probably busy." The matter-of-fact tone struck Tiffany as a little bit sad, but she kept the thought to herself. Haley scribbled a few lines and then obediently headed toward the bedroom.

Tiffany could have shouted with joy, but she didn't, just in case it might hamper the mood. This day called for a long, cozy nap.

***

An hour and a half later, her eyes opened whether she gave them permission or not. Her body protested, audibly, as in her joints creaking and popping, but she pushed the covers off gently and rose. Her youth meant nothing to muscles that hadn't found time to exercise in weeks. Haley slept next to her, one hand folded sweetly beneath a rosy cheek. Her thumb was stuck in her mouth, and Tiffany was glad she wasn't the one who'd have to break the charmer of that nasty habit.

She tiptoed out of the room and found her way back to the kitchen. A quick glance at her phone, and she paused. Her expectation that there would be a message had been so strong that when there wasn't one, she was confused. She put the phone back down and picked it up again, as if that would do it.

Her sister hadn't replied, and it was now four o'clock.

Tiffany texted again. Maybe the message hadn't gone through. Emma was probably frantic. Tiffany absentmindedly walked over to the living-room window. If her sister had driven over, she would have knocked. She also would have texted to let them know she'd arrived.

Hey, sis. If you don't text me soon, I'm going to call.

Restaurant policy discouraged the staff from receiving calls at work. The wait staff was expected to pay full attention to their customers, but Emma never worked this late on a Sunday afternoon. Her routine was set in concrete—work, take a nap with Haley, pick up groceries, and get ready for the week. Pain sliced her gut, the beginnings of panic.

Since texting didn't let her know whether a message was received, she thumbed down her screen and opened her social media. She typed in a quick *Where are you?* Then, for the heck of it, she snapped a picture of herself frowning and sent the unflattering picture to her sister before erasing the original.

Rather than have her neighbors think she was stalking them, she moved away from the window. She checked her texts again. Since getting her sister in trouble at work was one of the last things she wanted to do, she'd hold off as long as possible. Then, she did what any normal girl would do in a situation as dire as this. She called her mother.

Her mother answered on the second ring. Calling was the go-to for her mother. Tiffany didn't even know whether the older woman knew how to text. "Tiffany? Is something wrong?"

The question chilled her chest, as if her mother had rubbed ointment on it the way she'd done anytime they had the slightest symptom of a cold when they were little. Only now, her mother acted as if the only reason they'd talk was if there was something wrong. Then, the irony hit her. She had called because something might be wrong.

"Yes. Not that I only call when something's wrong." She talked fast, as if ripping off a Band-Aid. "But Emma's not answering her texts. Did she say anything to you about going somewhere this weekend?"

"No," her mother snapped. The question was sensitive, since her mother talked to her middle daughter rarely. "I haven't heard from her for weeks. You'd think that the way I sacrificed for you girls, the least she could do is call once in a while."

Tiffany kept her thoughts to herself about the many times her mother hadn't been there for her girls, especially for Emma. Even though her mother and father had cheated on each other, when Emma came home and said she was pregnant, the reaction hadn't been pretty.

"Why do you care if she isn't answering her texts?"

"I have Haley this weekend. You know, I babysit for Emma most weekends." The fact that Haley barely knew her grandmother was another point of contention. Her mother would say she didn't feel well enough to watch the child, but they all knew that seeing the child reminded her of the little girl's origins. "She wants to go home."

"Well, have you called Emma? Maybe something's wrong with her text function."

Tiffany choked on laughter. She would not mock her mother's lack of technological savvy. "I didn't want to get her in trouble at work." She hesitated, thinking she heard a sound coming from the bedroom. "I also don't know how long to wait before I start to worry."

"Worry? Worry about what?" Her mother might be hard on her daughters, but she could freak out with the best of them. "I don't think you should wait much longer. Call her at work."

There was a snort-sniffle combination coming down the hallway. "I want my mommy."

"Yes, ma'am," Tiffany said into the phone. "I have to go now. I'll call you back as soon as I get in touch with her."

"You do that." Her mother was talking even as Tiffany ended the call.

First order of business—she rushed to intercept the little girl trailing a stuffed bunny to match Tiffany's real bunny in the cage in the corner of her living room. Haley had her thumb entrenched in her mouth, crying around the appendage.

"Sweetheart." Despite the girl's weight and Tiffany's own slender frame, she scooped the girl up in her arms and carried her to the couch. "Haley, Aunt Tiffy's here. Your mommy is just working late. Don't worry."

Haley didn't say anything more; she just buried her face in Tiffany's chest and burrowed deep. Tiffany glanced at her phone behind her back. Nothing.

She inhaled a lot of oxygen and looked for strength she probably didn't have. So, next order of business, she needed to call her sister's work and see whether she'd volunteered for an extra shift, and she needed to do so without letting Haley hear her. If the child heard too much, she'd only get more upset.

"How about you watch some cartoons on my tablet?" Being a teacher meant she tried her best not to use technology as a babysitter, but when times got rough, the wimpy gave in.

Haley nodded, big crocodile tears pooling in her baby blues. "Yes, please."

Tiffany placed her phone on an end table where it couldn't fall into the black hole that was her couch. It took only a few minutes to grab the tablet off her desk in the other corner, opposite Bunny Foo Foo, who looked at her accusingly. She bent down and juggled the bag of rabbit chow.

Once she had Haley settled with a juice box and her favorite cartoon, she grabbed her phone and went into her bedroom. It took a few minutes of searching before the number scrolled by on her screen. When she hit call, her nerves skittered up and down with worry. The last thing she wanted to do was affect her sister's job, but she was running out of ideas.

"Jasmine's."

Tiffany hesitated but pushed herself to speak. "Hi. I'm sorry to bother you, but is Emma there?"

The hustle and bustle of a busy Italian restaurant sounded in the background. Just the thought of the place made Tiffany's stomach rumble with the idea of tomato sauce and meatballs. "Emma? No, she didn't show up for work today. No call, no show. She's fired."

Her appetite fled. Tiffany dropped her head into her free hand. "What if she's sick and couldn't come to the phone? Y'all don't even give her another chance?"

"Not when she hasn't shown up for work three days in a row."

Forget her appetite—her whole world flipped in an upside-down mess. "You mean she hasn't been there all weekend?"

CHAPTER 4

THE SILENCE ON THE OTHER end of the line wasn't deafening. She heard every miniscule sound: the heat pump whirring and rustling a loose piece of paper on her end table, the drip from the shower, the low buzz of the television in the next room.

"No." The tenor of the man's voice had an edge. "Wait. Do you think something's wrong? That's an entirely different story. Listen—who is this?"

"It's her sister. Tiffany."

"Let me get your name and number. I'll ask around. If I hear anything, if she told anybody anything, I'll call you. Okay?"

"Yes, thank you." Somehow, she managed to give the man, who turned out to be an assistant manager, the information. When he repeated it back to her, she said a quick "Thank you" and ended the call.

This made no sense. Her sister needed that job. She enjoyed the customers and the free food the staff often got to take home at the end of a shift.

After a few seconds of wasted time, she realized she was sitting on her bed, staring at her cell phone's blank screen. It would probably make Haley more than upset, but she needed to go to her sister's apartment. If there were any other way, she didn't have a clue. Wait.

She looked at recent calls and hit call back.

"Hey, Tiff." Her friend answered after one ring. "Twice in one day. Is something up?"

"Valerie." Her door remained closed. She couldn't stay back here much longer. Leaving a four-year-old alone, even in her living room, for any length of time, was not a good idea. "Yes, Emma's not answering my messages, and she didn't show up for work, all weekend."

"What?" Valerie dropped something and it clattered. "When's the last time you heard from her?"

Tiffany thought back. "Friday morning. We touched base to make sure I was going to pick Haley up from daycare."

"And she hasn't been heard from since?"

"Not by me or my mother. Or her job." Tiffany tried to picture Emma's friends, but so many of them disappeared after her pregnancy. "I need to go to her apartment and check to see if she's there. But I don't want Haley with me if something's wrong."

"Do you want to bring her here?" Valerie paused. "Or I can come over there—less disruption. I'm on my way. I just need to tell Travis."

Tiffany wanted to protest that she didn't want to be any trouble, but she squelched her polite nature.

"Thank you. I can't tell you how much I appreciate it."

"I'll just leave this sauce on simmer." Valerie talked more to herself than Tiffany. "Travis, I need you to watch so dinner doesn't burn. See you soon."

"Thanks again. I owe you one."

"No, you don't. Best-friend code. Bye."

Tiffany smiled for the first time in hours. Then, she raced into the living room to check on her niece. Who wasn't on the couch. Tiffany looked toward the ceiling, and by extension, heaven, in exasperation. "Why? Just why?"

"Aunt Tiffy," a little voice said from the kitchen. "Why are you saying 'Why?'"

Relief flooded her like a warm shower. Pivoting, she was confronted by a sight almost indescribable. Haley's pale little feet stuck out from behind the pantry door, but because of her angle, the rest of her was quite visible. She'd found the peanut butter and the chocolate-hazelnut spread and now resembled nothing more than a peanut-butter cup with both ingredients smeared all over her little body.

Tiffany almost cried out, "Why, oh Lord?" But she didn't because she'd have to explain everything, and she didn't know whether she could. Instead, laughter percolated and boiled right on over. "Oh my wow, Haley. How could you? What are you?"

"I was hungry." She was old enough to know better. "I didn't mean to make a mess, but when I spilled some on my shirt, then I couldn't get it off my shirt no matter how I tried. I didn't mean to."

Was it wrong to be happy that she now had a good excuse to go to Emma's apartment that didn't involve lying to Haley? The girl needed clean clothes, and there were no more spares here. Tiffany laughed until she remembered her sister was AWOL.

"Okay, Haley bug. Let's get you in the tub."

The guilt on the child's face barely showed through the peanut butter. "Yes, ma'am. I'm sorry."

She picked up the containers off the floor and mourned the loss of her favorite snack. It was all—every bit—gone. Perching her fingers on the girl's shoulder, she steered her toward the bathroom, and peeled her shirt off. "So, I'm going to go get some clean clothes from your apartment."

Haley was four, not dumb. "Where's Mama? She's supposed to pick me up."

She was back to either lying or terrifying the child. "Your mama's working late. I just talked to the people at her job."

"At Jasmine's?" Haley understood a lot. Tiffany would be wise to remember that fact. "Did you talk to Mr. Fred?"

"No, I talked to Jonah." The child nodded, which meant she recognized the man's name. Tiffany would stick as close to the truth as possible. "Anyway, Ms. Valerie's going to come stay with you."

"Can't I come pick out my clothes?" Her bottom lip poked out as far as it could go. "I want to go home."

"I'm sorry, but you can't." Tiffany hadn't known she could be so firm. Normally, she was the fun aunt who gave the kid back to her mama worn out and full of sugar. "Your mama isn't home." At least, she didn't know if she was. "And you can't stay there by yourself."

"I'm a big kid."

Tiffany lifted an eyebrow and pointed at a particularly large glob of peanut butter in the fine blond hair.

Her doorbell rang just as she pulled a wriggling little girl from the tub and blanketed her in a fluffy white towel. The fluffy white made her think of her neglected Foo Foo again.

"Mama." Haley escaped and ran down the hallway, somehow keeping the towel around her torso.

Tiffany closed her eyes. If it was Emma, which she highly doubted, that would solve a lot of problems. Haley would still be naked, but hey, there were dirty clothes left from yesterday.

One glance through the peephole dashed those hopes. Tiffany pasted on a smile, because she really was happy to see her generous friend, and opened the door. "Valerie. Thank you!"

The woman was five feet, one inch of continuous motion. "I know that smile. You were hoping it was someone else. Why, look at that sight for sore eyes. Haley, sweetheart, you look like an inside-out jelly roll."

Tiffany grinned. Haley twisted and turned, wondering out loud what an inside-out jelly roll looked like. She didn't protest when her aunt grabbed her car keys and slipped out the door.

The light that was her niece kept her going for several miles before reality slapped her upside the face. She was driving to the other side of Summer Creek, which admittedly wasn't far, to try to figure out why her sister hadn't bothered to pick up the daughter that occupied her whole world. She swerved and almost caused a wreck. Her hands shook as she righted the car.

It didn't make sense, and when things didn't make sense, that wasn't good.

She was driving from one unimposing brick-and-cream-vinyl-siding apartment complex to another. The only reason the two sisters didn't share an address was that their workplaces were on opposite sides of the small town that was known for being the originator of sweet tea. Tiffany needed to be at Azalea Elementary, named after the vivid flowers that blanketed the Low Country in the spring, at seven a.m. every weekday, including tomorrow. Her sister managed the offices of an insurance company closer to Charleston.

There were also the many, many differences between them that would have made living together a very bad idea.

Tiffany parked her average-looking four-door sedan, bought used, in the spot next to Emma's SUV. The presence of the vehicle, in light of her sister's lack of response, had her checking her phone again. Emma might have a vehicle with stickers that simultaneously advertised, "Baby on Board" and "If you can read this, flip me over," but she was a good mother.

Punching the button to lock her car, Tiffany raced down the stairwell to her sister's bottom-floor apartment. Without giving herself time to worry one more second, perhaps needlessly, she knocked three times.

When she didn't hear pounding footsteps, she rang the bell.

Nothing.

"Okay," she reassured herself. "There are many possible reasons."

She fiddled with her keys and located the spare her sister had illegally given her. So, sue them both. Her sister needed her.

Still, she glanced around and saw no one who might rat her out. The door opened, and she slid inside. The living room shone with tinsel and a cheap artificial tree with handmade ornaments, many with the telltale crooked lines but adorable signature of a toddler. Pictures of Haley perched on the bookshelves and hung on the wall. This was not the home of a woman who abandoned her child.

"Emma?" Tiffany made her way through the silent rooms. Nothing was disturbed; nothing was out of place. In the master bedroom, the comforter was smooth, and the decorative throw pillows were lined up. One of her theories had been a deathly ill sister who was so feverish she couldn't find her phone. Tiffany exhaled, trying to release her pent-up stress. She retraced her steps and went through Haley's pink room and the bathrooms. There was no sign of a struggle.

Jimbo's crate was empty. Emma could be walking the dog. Emma walked around the apartment, searching for some clue, until she could look no more. If Emma had been walking around the neighborhood, she'd have taken her phone with her.

Fifteen precious minutes passed. She forced a deep, calming breath, or she might hyperventilate. Pulling out her phone, she decided embarrassment was the better part of valor. If she made a fool of herself and her sister turned up in an hour, she'd live with the humiliation and move on.

"9-1-1." The dispatcher managed friendly and professional in a perfect combination. "What's the location of your emergency?"

"I'd like to report a missing person. I know it might be too early, but I don't know the rules," she stammered. "Wait—the location?" She swallowed. "Um, I'm at her apartment." Tiffany concentrated. Her sister's address didn't roll off her tongue. She'd driven here so often that the exact address escaped her. A glance around the room, and she found a stack of mail in a basket on the kitchen peninsula. "108 Brickyard Way, Apartment A, Summer Creek."

"Thank you." There were other voices in the background, but Tiffany hung on to the kindness in the woman on the other end of the line. "So, you say you're reporting a missing person. Who is she?"

"My sister. Emma Grace Marano."

"And when was the last known contact with Emma?"

"Friday." Tiffany riffled through her sister's mail basket, not having a clue what she hoped to find. "I spoke to her Friday. She hasn't shown up all weekend for her job, and she hasn't been in contact with her daughter."

Warning bells should have rung last night, but she'd taken Haley to a movie, and it had been too late for a video chat when they returned. Haley had fallen asleep in the movie and crashed in the car. Tiffany had carried the unconscious preschooler into the apartment and put them both to bed with only a quick text letting Emma know they'd gotten home safely. She'd been too busy this morning getting them dressed and out the door for church to realize Emma hadn't replied.

"Has she done something like this before?" The dispatcher sounded like she was running through a script.

"No." A chill raced down her body. "Never. She would never leave her daughter unless something was wrong."

The pause on the other end signaled that they'd crossed some line from probably a girl strung out on drugs somewhere to a possible missing-person case. "We'll have an officer there in just a few minutes. Please, identify yourself when you answer the door and keep your hands where the officer can see them."

Tiffany's throat constricted. This couldn't be real. "Yes, ma'am. I will."

"Goodbye. I hope you find your sister."

"Thank you," she said, her voice raspy. "Goodbye."

Tiffany stood in the middle of her sister's decorated-for-Christmas living room, frozen.

Since she hadn't moved and couldn't see a clock, it could have been minutes or hours before the doorbell rang. The sound made her squeal. For a bizarre heartbeat, she expected her sister to answer the door since it was her apartment, after all.

Then, her feet started moving of their own accord. She turned the door handle and found herself staring at a uniform-encased chest. When she looked up, the shock had her swaying in place.

"Nick?"

CHAPTER 5

NICK WALSH HAD BEEN A police detective for just a few months, an officer for two-plus years. Before that, he'd been a grunt in the US Marines, stationed in some pretty lousy crap holes. None of his experiences had prepared him for what faced him now.

"Tiffany?" His voice sounded thin, like it belonged to a boy whose voice hadn't changed yet. "Did you report a missing person?"

His heart couldn't handle seeing her twice in one day after so many years' absence, especially after how they'd left things. Or rather, how he'd left and she'd never bothered to write. They'd been more than high school sweethearts. She'd been his rock when his father left and his mother fell to pieces. He'd talked her down when her self-centered mother made her feel like a fire ant to be brushed off the skin and avoided at all costs.

"Um, yes, yes, I did." She didn't step aside to grant him entrance. "You're a cop?"

The humor of their less-than-intelligent questions had him grounded again. "Yes, yes, I am. Can I come in?"

He walked in and scanned the entire room. He saw nothing of Tiffany in this room with its dark sofa and chairs. He also needed to stop staring at those blue eyes that had figured heavily in his dreams the first couple of years apart.

"Oh, sorry. Sure." She walked backward and almost fell on top of the coffee table. The wooden edge must have cut into the curve of her calf, because she winced.

"Are you all right?" Years apart hadn't dampened his concern, and maybe they should have.

"Yeah." She rubbed her leg, making herself less than truthful. "Do you want to sit down?"

He sat on the love seat across from her, wanting distance but also needing to maintain eye contact. "Yes, please. And you sit down, too; try to relax a little. Most missing persons aren't missing at all. They just need a break from responsibilities or a bad relationship."

Tiffany set her shoulders back, alert and furious. "My sister isn't perfect, but she'd never just take a break without telling us. Something is wrong."

He forced his face to remain neutral by thinking of a sergeant yelling in his face. Otherwise, he'd react to the fire in her eyes and the color in those pale cheeks, and that would be inexcusable. The woman, no matter their past, had a beloved sister missing. "I'm not doubting you. I want you to have hope. Okay—start from the top. When did you last talk to her?"

"Friday, when she called me to make sure that I was going to pick up Haley and give me the pass code for the daycare."

He was watching the late-afternoon sun filter through her runaway blond hair when the words sank in.

"Haley is my niece. You met her this morning."

"Yes, I did. Wait—she's your niece?" He tore his eyes away from the straight hair that always tangled, no matter how hard she tried. Somehow, he was relieved that she didn't share a child with another man and, in the next second, realized how ridiculous that relief was.

"Yes, Emma's daughter. So, you now understand why my sister wouldn't just take off. Haley is her everything. I only watch her on the weekends when Emma works at her waitressing job. Our other sister, Shelby, watches her one weekend a month, and Emma has one weekend off." Tiffany almost pushed herself between the couch cushions, away from him.

"Busy woman," he said, focusing on the missing sister and his job. He pulled out his phone and started taking notes. "Have you called Shelby?"

Tiffany paused, and he could tell she hadn't. "No." She shook her head. "Shelby went out of town with some girlfriends from her fitness group. They're in a cabin and off the grid. I did call Mama, and she has no idea." The phone in her hand buzzed and captured her attention. Her expression was resigned when she faced him again. "That was nothing. A text message from a friend. I also called Emma's manager earlier, and she didn't show up for work all weekend. They're going to fire her."

"Friends? Boyfriend?"

"She doesn't have either, as far as I know. I mean, she had friends—lots of them—before Haley, but now, she doesn't really have time. Not for close friends." She finally leaned toward him, her shower of blonde hair covering her face.

Nick's fingers hovered over the screen as he tried to reconcile the description with the younger sister he'd known—the blonde cheerleading gymnast who'd walked the halls of Summer Creek High as if they'd been her personal runway. She'd been a complete contrast to the sweet mouse who'd been his girl.

"So, she doesn't go out? Keep in touch with high school friends?" Even he, the military brat who'd moved to town as a freshman and never really fit into one of the long-established groups, had a couple of buddies he'd looked up once he and Elloree moved back in with his mom and stepdad temporarily. His parents had retired to be near the beach, and this was their forever home, but it hadn't been that way for most of his childhood.

Tiffany's pale pink lips pressed together. She'd changed from the crisp white blouse and dark skirt she'd been wearing at church into a Walk for Babies T-shirt and jeans. She'd always dressed modestly to go with her shy nature, another stark contrast to both her outgoing sisters.

"No." She ducked her head. "When she got pregnant in her first year at Lowcountry Tech, she'd already started losing touch with friends from high school. They'd gone to the bigger schools or four-year colleges, and it wasn't cool to go to community college. Then, she dropped out, and they stopped messaging her when she no longer had a future."

He waited for the appropriate words to come to him, but his brain didn't supply them. Finally, he settled for an ineffective, "I'm sorry."

"Thank you." Her small nose and large eyes relaxed a bit, as if he'd managed to say the right thing, after all. "So, what do you think?"

He'd had two trains of thought battling for dominance all day. One had him focusing on the here and now, but thoughts of her would pass on the right. And as of now, he had no ideas. He scanned his notes, considering the evidence. A third possible way of thinking crossed his mind. He stared at the face that he'd carried with him in some pretty nasty places to help him make it through and shook his head. "I think it's too soon to know. I need more information, though. Remind me of her hair color, eyes, height, any tattoos or piercings. It's been a while."

Anger flashed behind those baby blues, a new phenomenon from what he remembered, but she took a deep breath, and her expression switched to neutral. "Yes, yes, it has."

He stared at her, at a loss for words. She'd been the one to break her promise. She'd never written. Not once. Tiffany acted as if he'd betrayed her. That wasn't possible, since he'd waited a full two years before moving on and dating someone else.

"Same height as me, five-foot-four; blond hair, a little curlier than mine; same blue eyes. She got a tattoo above her ankle in high school, with the other cheerleaders. *SC* for *Summer Creek*."

If Emma had a tattoo, the girl must have been on the road to rebellion since their family had been very conservative. He pushed aside memories. "Do you have a current picture of her?"

Tiffany turned in a slow circle. "This is her apartment, not mine. There has to be."

Her voice dwindled. The walls, the end tables—all held photos of Haley. "This is her apartment?" Nick pushed himself to his feet. The disconnect between the Tiffany he'd known and the almost-gothic decor made sense now. "Did you notice anything disturbed?"

She blinked as if she struggled to keep up. There was so much more he needed to ask. For one thing, they sat in the missing woman's apartment, and he hadn't even searched the rooms. He'd been too busy staring at the woman across from him.

"Nothing. I can show you around." She started to rise, as if she would walk with him.

He held out a hand. "Why don't you relax for a few minutes? I'm just going to look around and see if anything stands out."

"Oh." She lowered herself back down and shrank against the couch cushions.

He wanted more than anything to wrap her in his arms and tell her that everything would be okay, but somehow, he'd lost that privilege years ago. He started walking.

The apartment was small, and not a thing looked out of place. There was no sign of struggle and no sign of hurried packing. The blouses and dresses in the closet were evenly spaced out, so no grabbing, and a large suitcase took up the back half of the walk-in. Even her toothbrush was perched in a cup on the side of the sink. So, she might have used an overnight bag with an extra set of toiletries, but she hadn't planned on being gone long if she'd left of her own accord. Nothing said she hadn't—or at least, not inside the apartment. He needed more information. He retraced his steps to the living room. "What kind of car does she drive?"

"You can see for yourself." Tiffany sat where he'd left her, her slender body curled in on itself, phone cradled in her lap.

Her words sent shock waves through him. He'd been very much leaning toward an overworked young mother taking off for a much-needed vacation. "What?"

"Her vehicle is right downstairs." Why had she not mentioned this before? Why had he not asked?

"Show me, please." This rewrote the entire scenario. His nerves stood on edge the way they'd done back in Afghanistan when the sirens sounded.

"Okay." Tiffany pushed herself to a stand as if she'd suddenly aged a lot. "Do you want to go out there or just look through the window?"

"Let's walk outside." He needed fresh air. Even the smell of her honeysuckle perfume had him distracted. "I'll need the names of the businesses she worked for and the daycare." The daycare workers were the last known to have seen her. Tiffany wouldn't even know what clothes her sister had been wearing.

"Sure." She rattled off the names as she locked the door behind them. He typed and followed her lead to the parking lot. He managed to pay attention to the stairwell walls and the small landing, where bicycles were parked beneath the stairs. Nothing said that anything wrong had happened here. This was a safe place to live, and the bicycles with only cheap chain locks said people didn't fear theft.

The sport utility vehicle did not shout "single mother." There was a car seat in the back, and there was an identical one in the much-safer sedan parked next to it. He didn't need to ask to identify the car as Tiffany's. It shouted, "unassuming elementary schoolteacher who loved kids and poured everything into her babies, including her niece."

He walked around and searched the periphery. Again, there was no sign of a struggle, which didn't mean much since a strong man could grab a small woman and not leave a single clue behind. Still, if she'd fought, something could have fallen from her purse, or she could have left behind a scarf. Nothing.

Tiffany's phone vibrated. Someone bothered to place an actual phone call. He wavered between wanting to hear and not wanting to eavesdrop if the call turned personal and irrelevant to the case. He settled on going back to stand near the driver's side and staring at the ground.

"That was Jasmine's."

Tears pooled at the corner of her eyes. The need to hold her overwhelmed him, and with anyone else, he might have followed the urge; police officers were allowed to show compassion. Ex-boyfriends didn't enjoy that privilege. "I hear the chicken marsala is fantastic." He opted for the dry humor that would hopefully provide a distraction.

Her shoulders shook in a minimal laugh. She sank to the curb, her legs folding. He rushed over to prop her up before she hit the concrete.

"One of the waitresses said Emma had been talking to some guy online. They were going to meet," she said in a broken and bruised voice.

He held her as she sobbed.

When the storm started to abate, he released her and backed away. He needed the distance. "Tiffany, she could still be fine. There's no way to know if the man was a complete stranger or someone she knew from school. Right now, I need to know—where's Haley?"

She sniffed and swiped at her tears with her forearm. "At my apartment. Valerie's watching her. Didn't I tell you that already?"

"No, you didn't." He kept any reaction to her mistake out of his tone. "That's okay. Now, it's about time for dinner. Are you okay to drive home and eat?"

"But Emma."

"Emma isn't here. There's nothing either of us can do right now that would keep us from food." He gave her the side grin she used to love, if she remembered. The food quote had also been one of their things. His girl might have been shy, but she could devour some French fries. "When you feel up to driving, I want you to concentrate on nothing but taking care of yourself and that little girl. There will be a lead investigator, and he'll be in touch with you tomorrow. I'll be in touch if anything happens sooner."

She braced her hands on her knees and straightened her shoulders. "I never gave you my phone number."

"No, you didn't. May I have it? And Emma's? I need that as soon as possible."

"I tried calling, but she didn't answer." The ordeal must be wearing on her if she didn't understand that the police would want to track her sister's phone.

"I understand. We're going to try pinging her phone. If she's made any calls, the cell-phone towers can triangulate and give us a good idea of where she might be, if her phone is turned on."

"Oh." She closed her eyes and opened them again to look at him straight on. "I don't have her number memorized." She searched her contacts for the number.

They exchanged information, and he helped her to her feet. Her purse swung at her side, narrowly missing him, and it must have equaled a third of her body weight. "What do you have in that thing? Rocks?"

She gave him the ghost of a smile. "You know, your wife must have one of these. Women carry their whole lives in their purses."

He paused at the mention of his wife and wondered why she'd bring up a woman she'd never met. Her gaze flickered to his wedding ring and away. Awareness rang through him. He needed to tell her about Lynna, but he didn't know whether this was the time. Her focus was on her missing sister, where it should be. "Yeah, yeah, they do. Are you going to be okay to drive?"

He could offer to escort her home if she was too distraught, but somehow, that felt like overstepping his bounds in this case.

"Yes." Again, she shoved her shoulders back as if she would face down the world and win. In some ways, she was the Tiffany he knew better than he knew himself, and in some ways, the seven intervening years really mattered. "I'll be fine. Thank you. Please, call me soon."

He rested a hand on her shoulder to comfort one or both of them. "You do the same. Be safe, Tiffany."

"Good night."

He watched as she drove away. She owned a single-woman car and didn't wear a ring. It was more than he could have hoped for, but he didn't know whether it would matter. If something terrible had happened to Emma, Tiffany wouldn't be in the market for rehashing an old romance. She'd be grieving for quite some time and, from the looks of things, probably thrust into the role of mothering her sister's child.

He didn't know whether he could attend the same church and live in the same town without touching her. For everyone's sake, especially Emma's and Haley's, he prayed that her sister had made yet another bad decision and would tell them all about it when she got back home.

He stood there and prayed for a few minutes before the cold had him squaring his shoulders and unlocking his squad car. He had a missing person to find.

CHAPTER 6

TIFFANY DROVE ON AUTOPILOT, BUT she made it home in one piece. As soon as she walked in the door, Valerie met her eyes, and Tiffany shook her head. Her friend just pressed her lips together in a tight, straight line and studied the floor for a few minutes. This was definitely a case of no news is bad news.

Haley bolted toward the door like a beagle trying to run down the street and chase cars. Her eyes were big, and her mouth wide open. All that was missing were the lolling tongue and floppy ears, even though the flying hair could substitute. Tiffany held out her arms and suffered through the deep disappointment when the girl realized it was only her.

"Where's Mama?" She might be devastated at the wrong person entering the door, but she held on to her aunt with her little arms as if they were ropes. "Is she still at work?"

Tiffany looked at her friend, but Valerie refused to meet her eyes. There was no good answer. She couldn't keep lying to the little girl, or she'd in essence have been abandoned by the two most important adults in her life at the same time. Desperate, Tiffany prayed for help. Peace flowed through her, but it got followed too quickly by ever-present worry. "Hey, Haley. Let's sit on the couch."

The child had a grip on her legs and wouldn't let go. Normally, this would be a game, and Tiffany would drag her across the floor, both of them giggling. Today, she just got them across the room the best she could. When she peeled the little fingers off her so she could sit, Haley released her only long enough to let go and then jumped in her lap.

"Haley, I want to apologize." The girl waited. "Earlier, I said your mom was working late, and it wasn't true. I've never lied to you before, and I promise not to lie to you again."

She might regret the promise, but right was right.

"You lied to me?" The nose that was a little too long for the small face scrunched up like a hair ornament. "Why? Mama ain't at work?"

Tiffany rubbed the little girl's back without thinking. She would give anything to make everything perfect in her little world. "No, she hasn't been at work all weekend. I don't know where she is."

"Is she okay?"

This is where she could fudge the truth and hope to God—no, scratch that; have faith in God—that the words would become truth if they weren't already. "I think so. I trust God to take care of her. Will you pray with me?"

Haley bobbed her head up and down. Her hair fell across her cheeks and stuck to the tears she'd been crying. Tiffany wiped the matted strands back from her face. She closed her eyes and then opened one of them to see whether Haley had followed suit. She had, in her trusting, innocent way. Tiffany felt a hand on her shoulder. She'd forgotten all about Valerie.

"Dear Lord, thank You for letting us come to You in prayer. Thank You for Your Son, who died on the cross for us because He loved us so much. We know You love us, and we know You love Emma. Wherever she is, please keep her safe, and please bring her home to us soon. Amen."

"Amen." Valerie's voice was low and solemn. She squeezed Tiffany's shoulder and walked into the kitchen. She put her coat on and her purse on her shoulder. "I'm heading out. If you need anything—anything at all—don't hesitate to call me."

Tiffany snuffled when she inhaled, intending nothing more than replying. The tears had sneaked up on her. "Thank you," she managed. "I will. Thank you for watching her tonight."

Valerie ruffled Haley's hair as she took a detour to the couch before making her way to the door. "And, Tiff. Don't try to do everything. Call in sick tomorrow if you need to; you never miss. Give yourself some time to work this out. It's the last week of classes before Christmas break. It's not like you'll be getting a lot of teaching done anyway."

Missing work would never have occurred to her. It was probably a good idea, given that she'd need to talk to the other police detective and figure out a way to get to school on time and drop off Haley at a daycare across town. "Okay."

"Bye." Valerie left but not before glancing Haley's way one last concerned time.

Haley sat in Tiffany's lap, head in the curve of her aunt's shoulder, for some time. Tiffany held her, waiting for the little girl to make the next move. She knew they needed dinner. She'd grabbed several outfits and a fresh pair of pajamas, but there was the puzzle of what to do with the hours between now and bedtime. She was a teacher, so setting the child in front of the television hit her all wrong, but they'd done everything she'd planned in the allotted time slots.

If Emma didn't come home soon, there would be a lot of empty time slots.

"I'm hungry."

"Okay." Tiffany wrapped the little girl's long legs around her waist and piggybacked her the few steps it took to reach the kitchen counter. Even though it violated her own rules, she set Haley on the counter. "Now, let's see what we've got in the fridge."

Somehow, they managed to fill the time. There was spaghetti to make and dishes to wash and put away. There was a bath to be had and books to be read. They drew funny pictures and practiced the sounds of letters sung to a weird tune that helped make it fun. When Tiffany tucked Haley into bed, the little girl prayed for her mama, but she didn't cry.

They'd both convinced themselves that God would take care of Emma.

Heaven help everyone, especially the little girl's budding faith, if God had let the broken world and her sister's stupid decisions lead to a different conclusion.

Tiffany flipped on the hall light and made her way into the living room. She didn't know where the anger came from, but her whole body started shaking. If her sister hadn't been abducted—and every syllable stabbed her like needles hidden in a carpet—then she had done something so awful that Tiffany didn't know whether she could forgive her. And where would that leave them?

Forcing air out of her lungs and a little of the bitterness from always being the good child and having to pick up the pieces, she padded over to the desk where her phone was charging. She swiped the screen with her thumb.

Still nothing. No news was worse than bad news—it was terrifying and not fair and wrong.

Her Bible lay on the desk, and she rested her palm on the cover. There were words of comfort there, and she'd be better off when she let go of this bitterness and recognized that she was no more good than anyone else, even Emma, but she wasn't there yet.

Right now, she wanted to pursue another way of searching. The police had their resources, but she had the internet. It took only a few seconds, and she was logged into her laptop. Earlier, she'd messaged her sister and still hadn't received an answer. Hoping, even though she was starting to think of hope as stupid, she clicked on the necessary buttons to see that the message had been delivered but not read. She exhaled with some force. It had been wishful thinking.

She went to her sister's page and scrolled down. Emma hadn't posted anything since Thanksgiving. Frantic now, since she'd so hoped for clues, she went through her sister's history as to whose stuff she'd liked or any pictures that might offer a suggestion as to who the man she'd met online might have been.

Nothing. There was nothing helpful on any account. The only things she'd pinned online were some wedding gowns, decorations for a little girl's room, and a recipe for rocky-road brownies.

Tiffany dropped her head into one hand and slumped against the back of the cheap garage-sale desk chair. She'd run out of ideas.

With no more avenues to pursue a sister who had obviously not shared a great deal with her, she let herself be sucked in by the internet. She clicked on her friend Danielle's ultrasound picture of her baby at six months and her coworker Bruce's picture of his new truck. She kept supporting person after person until she reached pictures she'd already seen. Beaten, she gave in and pursued the second reason her brain had pushed her body into this corner.

She searched for information on Nick. It was all public. They'd been friends on every type of social media available when he drove off into the sunset, but at some point—maybe a year after no word from him—she'd blocked him. It had been childish, yes, but it had felt so good.

She rescinded the block.

He was worse than her sister. He hadn't posted anything in years. The lack of Elloree pictures baffled her. If she had a daughter, she'd crash the internet with pictures of everything from first tooth to first steps to a grin that was slightly different from the hundreds before. His profile description included "Married to Lynna Johnston." Her finger hovered over the pad of her laptop, but she hesitated. Why was she needlessly torturing herself?

She knew better, but she pressed down, and the page blinked to life. Lynna had been in the Marines, too. She stood in a line of marines, strong and confident, everything Tiffany had never been. There were pictures of her and Nick, just the two of them, grinning and laughing in their olive-green T-shirts and camouflage pants. There were pictures of her pregnant in civilian clothes, a pretty yellow dress to go with her deep tan. Tiffany couldn't tan; she only burned, driving across town, looking out a window.

Lynna's posts stopped a little over four years ago, about the time Elloree was born.

Why would they both stop posting when the barrage should have begun? They might have divorced, but that wouldn't explain the complete lack of pictures. A worse thought occurred to her. Something might have happened to Lynna, but there was nothing to indicate a tragedy.

Her cell phone buzzed, and she exited the page. He was married, they didn't post pictures, and she needed to move on with her life. Again.

Nick had texted her. I JUST WANTED TO LET YOU KNOW THAT HAROLD PHELPS WILL BE CALLING YOU IN THE MORNING. I'M OFFICIALLY OFF THE CASE. SO, I CAN SAY JUST HOW SORRY I AM THAT YOU'RE GOING THROUGH THIS.

She flinched, with guilt and maybe disgust at just how eagerly she'd read his message. THANK YOU.

Nick: IF YOU NEED ANYTHING, LET ME KNOW.

I APPRECIATE IT. She should say something more, but she'd just seen the evidence that he was off limits, even though she was more confused than ever. GOOD NIGHT.

Nick: GOOD NIGHT.

She almost put the phone down, but he wasn't done texting.

Nick: WAIT. I HAVE TICKETS TO THE DEWEES ISLAND CHRISTMAS CARNIVAL FOR NEXT SATURDAY. DO YOU AND HALEY WANT TO COME?

Her heart leaped, and she mentally yelled at it. The horror of making plans as if her sister wasn't ever coming back had her shivering. Going somewhere with him would be inappropriate, except she would need to keep Haley occupied as much as possible. It was on the tip of her fingers to ask whether his wife was coming, but she couldn't bring herself to do it. There was something there. The Nick she knew would never go somewhere with another woman if he was still married. On the third hand that didn't exist, this was, in the end, nothing more than a playdate for these two girls. She was so confused.

He was waiting for an answer.

Tiffany: YES, IF EMMA'S NOT BACK.

Nick: MAYBE EVEN IF SHE IS. SHE'S OKAY, TIFFANY. I HAVE TO BELIEVE IT. YOU DO, TOO.

His faith shored her up like a steady hand. She blinked back tears before texting back. I DO. THANK YOU. SEE YOU ON SATURDAY.

Nick: SIX O'CLOCK. WE'LL TAKE THE GIRLS FOR DINNER BEFOREHAND?

Tiffany: YES. SIX. GOOD NIGHT.

Her answers had grown choppy. The day had caught up with her. She dropped her head into her hands and almost drifted off to sleep right there at her desk. Hopefully, she'd wake up in the morning, and they'd all get a do-over.

Except for her plans for next Saturday night.

GOOD NIGHT. GOD BLESS, he'd texted back.

CHAPTER 7

THE PHONE RANG.

Emma's number appeared on the screen.

Tiffany splattered toothpaste all over her mirror. She dropped the battery-powered toothbrush in the sink, still running, and grabbed her phone. Her stomach rolled, and she swiped with her thumb. "Answer; answer."

"Tiffany?" Crackles and pops inserted themselves between the syllables. "It's…"

The name got drowned out by the bad connection, but Tiffany didn't need to hear the word. She recognized her sister's voice, barely. "Emma, you're alive? Emma, we've been so worried."

"—okay. We're safe but can't…" What could have been the sound of a train roaring in the background cut off whatever would have followed.

"Wait—we? Who's we?"

"I don't think I can talk long on this phone." For some reason, those words came through loud and clear. "—car broke down. I forgot…charger." Every sentence gave the impression that English was her sister's third language.

"—back soon... can't say." What couldn't she say? How soon was soon? "—as I can."

"Emma, I need to ask about Haley." Tiffany's heart raced, trying to catch up with her sister in the distance.

"Tell her...love." The sound of engines—many of them, as in a motorcycle convention—drowned out Emma's voice. "—running out. So sorry. Bye."

The phone went dead.

Tiffany stared at the faithless machine, needing someone or something to blame, even though she was certain her end of the line hadn't been at fault.

Anger ripped through her. Hours—days—had passed with no word, and her sister couldn't even manage a clear phone call. She leaned against the sink and swayed back and forth, fighting the tears. She needed to let people know that Emma was safe, alive.

Haley had been asleep for hours. It was after midnight, and her mother's routine was rigid. She would have gone to sleep at ten o'clock. Nick had been back in her life only one day.

She didn't even know when she should call the police and let them know to forget about it. Her self-centered sister had called to let them know she was safe. She was somewhere, coming back sometime, and was with an unknown someone.

She was safe. Tiffany closed her eyes and swayed where she stood.

Fear, followed by amazing relief, was beyond exhausting.

Beyond what she could have hoped for.

CHAPTER 8

"AUNT TIFFY." HALEY STOOD NEXT to her bed, stuffed bunny in hand, tears running down the side of her little nose. "I want my mommy."

Tiffany located her bedside clock through bleary eyes. She was glad she kept the traditional machine, because right now, she had no idea where her phone might be or whether it had any remaining charge after last night's marathon of call after call. The last call echoed in her head, and she jerked upright. "Haley."

The girl double sniffled. "What?"

Tiffany shoved the covers off her and dragged the little girl onto her lap and into a hug. "Your mama called last night. She's okay. She's okay, sweetheart."

The child burst into serious sobbing. "She's okay. Mama."

Tiffany rubbed small circles on Haley's back and waited.

Haley pushed back and stared. "Where is she? When can I go home?"

The bright blue eyes had a grown-up edge that intimidated Tiffany. "I don't know. The call was garbled."

"Why?"

Tiffany inhaled, her breath hard edged. She could strangle her sister for putting them through this. Why hadn't she let them know she was going out of town, and why hadn't she called before they got to the point of worry? "Good question, Haley bug. I don't know why. Let's ask your mama when she gets back."

Haley jumped off the bed and threw down her toy. "When?"

"I don't know." Tiffany was seriously getting tired of those words.

"You don't know anything, do you?" Haley ran out of the room, the flounce on her nightgown kicking up as she went.

Her niece wasn't wrong.

Tiffany closed her eyes. Then, panic struck. She had overslept. This was her last week of classes before break, but she did have class. One hour. She had one hour to eat, get dressed, and get to school before the first bell rang, and she had a child to drop off at daycare.

She had never moved so fast in her life.

The day passed in an agonizing, slow blur. When she picked up Haley from the daycare that evening, the child's face contorted with anger and disappointment and more emotions than a four-year-old should possess.

"Where's Mama?"

"I don't know."

Tuesday night, Tiffany put her tote bag full of papers to be graded on the kitchen table and fed Foo Foo; then, the doorbell rang. When she didn't open the door within a nanosecond of the bell ringing, the person on the other side pounded as if she didn't believe the doorbell functioned properly.

"Mama." Tiffany didn't peep through the peephole; she just swung the door wide and pasted on a neutral expression since a smile at this point would be a flat-out lie.

Her five-foot-if-she-was-lucky mother barged through the door, purse first. Six steps in, she stopped in the middle of the living room and peered at the corners. "Where's that granddaughter of mine? She must be devastated, poor thing."

Tiffany froze in the open doorway, glancing around the room for some clue that the world had come to an end. It took a few seconds of cold air on her back and a relatively clean living room to reassure her that the world was still turning on its normal axis. She closed the door. "She's in the back bedroom. Haley!"

Her mother frowned, and Tiffany was surprised when she didn't fuss at her for using her outdoor voice inside. Instead, her mother turned to loop her purse over one of the kitchen-table chairs. The small apartment got a bit smaller.

Haley skidded to a stop at the end of the hallway.

"You poor child, come and hug your Meemaw Hudson." Her mother held out her arms and stormed forward as if to envelop the little girl in a bear hug. Haley ducked beneath the coming onslaught and almost knocked Tiffany down with the force of her escape.

"Why, not in my whole life have I ever." Tiffany's mother clicked her tongue.

Tiffany rested a hand on Haley's shoulder, her fingers twitching. "I'm sorry, Mom. I think she's a bit skittish, with everything going on."

"With her own grandmother?" She made a move to grab her purse.

"Mama." Tiffany held out a hand to stop her mother from leaving, if that were possible. "Why don't you sit down, and I'll make some coffee? Maybe if you give Haley a few minutes."

She wouldn't make promises for her niece, but it meant something that her mother was here. A few tense seconds passed while her mother patted her freshly curled hair and adjusted her glasses, and Tiffany held her breath.

"Okay." Her mother sighed and released her purse strap. She pulled out a chair and lowered her heavyset body. "But I want a lot of that hazelnut creamer you keep. It's a bit late in the day for coffee. If I have too much, I won't sleep."

"Yes, ma'am." Tiffany pried Haley's fingers from her blouse and led her to the chair across from her grandmother. She wouldn't force the child to hug someone she didn't want to, but Haley could talk. "Would you like some hot chocolate, Haley? I got the caramel kind."

Haley's head whipped around to follow her progress, and her eyes lit up. "Yes, please. The caramel kind is the best."

"Caramel kind it is." Tiffany walked around the kitchen island and scrambled for the makings of coffee and hot chocolate. "So, Mom. How's Jim doing?"

"Oh, he's working all the time, and I hardly ever see him. I get real lonely in that house by myself. You'd think my daughters would come by and visit more often, given how close you all are. It's not even a ten-minute drive from here." Her mother had retired over a decade ago, and the years seemed to have affected her memory as to what it meant to work full time. On the other hand, they could all visit more.

"I'm sorry," Tiffany said, telling herself not to keep count as to just how many times she apologized in one visit. "After Friday, my schedule should open up for Christmas. I thought we might go shopping next week. We could even go to that teahouse you like for lunch."

Her mother started crying. "I don't know that I can go shopping with Emma missing. She and I might not see eye to eye, but she's still my daughter. How could she do this to me?"

Haley's eyes got wider and wider, stretching the limits of her little face.

"Mama." Tiffany turned on the coffeepot and carried the tea kettle to the sink for water. "Emma is okay. She called and let me know she's safe."

"But she didn't call me." Her mother dug in her purse for a tissue. Tiffany raced over to the end table by the couch and grabbed the box. "She didn't even think of her own mother, that I might be worried."

Tiffany's throat went dry. "Mama." She pulled a chair over where she could sit next to the older woman and rubbed her back. "I think she could only make one phone call. Her phone was running out of charge. She forgot her charger and was worried about Haley."

The little girl had her hands in her lap, fingers twisting. She was too young for this.

"She couldn't find another phone in all this time?" Her mother, now Mrs. Hudson after her third marriage—two since Tiffany's father—whipped the words out in accusation. "There is an internet, where she could message her own mother. I have an email account. There's no excuse."

Haley's mouth started to quiver.

"Haley, hon, why don't you go to your room and play?" Tiffany kept her voice calm, even though every other part of her teetered on the edge. "I'll come get you when the hot chocolate is ready."

"No. I came to see her," her mother said. "She can sit here for five minutes, can't she?"

Haley whimpered.

She reached over and patted Haley's arm. "I'm sorry your mama disappeared like this. I'm sure everything will be okay. And don't you worry—if something bad happens, you always have a place to stay at my house. Family is family, after all."

Big tears streamed down the child's face. "I don't need a place to stay!" She jumped out of her chair. "My mama's coming back soon! Aunt Tiffy said so, and you're a mean old woman."

Tiffany reached out to stop the fleeing child. But the kid could duck and dodge with the best of them. She skirted both women's outstretched hands and ran down the hall before words found their way past Tiffany's lips.

"Oh, wow." She stood.

"Did you hear what she said to me? Calling me mean after I offered to take care of her." The purse was off the arm of the chair. "Children these days. You need to be careful, or that child will be trouble when she gets older—mark my words."

"Mama, why don't you wait?" Tiffany didn't know whether she could get Haley to apologize, but she didn't want her mother driving in this state. "Drink some coffee, and we'll talk."

"No, no." Her mother shook her head. "I'm not staying where I'm not wanted. 'Mean old woman.' You need to raise her better, or you'll be sorry."

The door shut behind her just as the tea kettle sang.

Tiffany covered her face with both hands. "She's not even my child."

***

Wednesday night, Tiffany felt like she had been run over by a sleigh, and the week was only half done. On the drive home, Haley was too quiet.

"How was your day, sweetie?" Tiffany asked, not knowing whether she wanted to hear the answer. If some kid had picked on her niece today, she might turn this car around.

"Fine." Haley picked at the belt on her car seat. "Is my mom picking me up tonight?"

Tiffany shut her eyes, which was a very bad idea when driving in bumper-to-bumper traffic. She opened them fast, but her answer didn't change. "I don't know."

"When will you stop saying that?" The little girl choked out the words, somewhere between yelling and a sob.

"I don't know," Tiffany whispered. "I'm sorry, Haley. I'd fix it if I could, but I can't. Maybe we can make some Christmas fudge when we get to the apartment?"

Haley glared at her in the rearview mirror. Yeah, candy wouldn't make it better, and they were both going to end up fat. It was a school night. They couldn't afford to go to the movies, and Tiffany couldn't wave a wand and make Emma appear.

By the time she got the girl to bed, they'd had two more yelling matches and one time-out—for Tiffany, not Haley. Tiffany had taken a break and sent herself to her room before she did something she'd regret, like spank a child who was already hurting.

She tucked the child into bed, prayed over her, and kissed her. "Good night, Haley bug. I love you. Don't ever forget that, even when we get mad at each other."

"I love you, too, Aunt Tiffy." Haley pushed herself up on her elbows and puckered up. Tiffany presented her cheek. The soft kiss lingered as she walked to the door and turned out the light. The glow of the unicorn night-light made the child out to be a cherub. "Sweet dreams, bug."

"Sweet dreams, Aunt Tiffy."

Tiffany drew a deep breath and almost closed the door, leaving a gap in case Haley called out in the middle of the night, which she had been doing the last few nights. She made her way into the living room, picking up toys and socks along the way.

Bunny Foo Foo sat in his cage, well fed for once, since petting him had been part of her self-punishment.

Her phone buzzed on her desk.

Nick: Can I come over? Mom made a casserole.

CHAPTER 9

TIFFANY FLOPPED DOWN ON THE floor, crisscross applesauce. Just the word *casserole* in the context of someone bringing it over to her house made her leg muscles weak. WHAT?

Nick: WOW. I DIDN'T REALIZE HOW THAT SOUNDED. EMMA'S OKAY, TIFFANY. BELIEVE IT. MOM JUST WANTED TO DO SOMETHING NICE FOR YOU SINCE YOU'RE GOING THROUGH A HARD TIME.

Tiffany sucked in a deep breath. Truth was truth. YES. HALEY'S ASLEEP. IT'S A GOOD TIME TO DROP BY.

Nick: ELLOREE'S ASLEEP, TOO. BE THERE IN FIFTEEN.

She started running around like a crazy woman. The number of shoes in the hallway alone defied belief. There were crumbs left on the table from their hurried dinner because homework had been more important than cleaning up.

She shoved stuff into the hall closet and shut the door, just barely avoiding slamming it in her rush. The dirty socks she'd gathered went into the hamper in the bathroom. She caught a glimpse of herself in the mirror and moaned. There was a reason people stayed home in the middle of the week.

Her lips were pursed, and she was in the middle of swiping pale pink lipstick on when a gentle knock echoed through the apartment. Here was a man who understood what it meant when a kid was asleep. She ran to answer before he was forced to knock again.

She swung open the front door. "Hey."

"Hey, yourself." His side grin said he liked what he saw, and nausea churned in her stomach.

He still wore the ring, and she'd just put makeup on for his arrival. What had she been thinking?

"Can I come in?" He held up a blue stoneware dish, not plastic, which meant she'd have to find a way to get the dish back to him no matter what. "I come bearing Mama's shrimp casserole."

He was being a thoughtful old friend—that's what this was. She waved an arm and stepped out of the way. "Please, and be sure to thank your mother for me. It's really hard to do everything and find time to cook."

"Tell me about it." He went straight to her kitchen. "Sorry it's too late for you to eat it tonight. I didn't get off shift until late. Mama about had my hide, but I figured you could put it in the fridge and reheat at will."

Tiffany nodded. "That sounds wonderful. Um, can I get you something? Cup of coffee?"

He emerged from the refrigerator and straightened. "I'd like that, and then, if you don't mind, could we talk?"

Tiffany licked lips that were suddenly dry. "Um, yeah, of course. It will just take a few minutes to get the pot going."

"That's fine." He walked past her into the living room. The kitchen and living room were one medium-sized room in her small two-bedroom apartment. There was normally plenty of space, even with Haley and her stuff that seemed to invade every corner.

She realized she was watching him while he stared at some pictures on her end table. Heat rushed to her cheeks, and she got busy making coffee for him, tea for her. The need for small talk, to find anything at all to say, pushed at her. "How was your day?"

He picked up a frame. "Haley is one well-loved child. My day was fine—a few speeding tickets, one possible fraud case. Nice and boring."

She dropped the carton of cream on the counter, splashing a white droplet trail on the brown granite. What he didn't say—what he had implied whether purposefully or not—was that there were days when his job wasn't so mundane. "Well, that's good. Can you tell me about the fraud case? Or do you have to keep things like that secret?"

"If it's an ongoing case, I can't say too much, just that it's an old, established business trying to make a potentially fraudulent insurance claim. It would hurt the community if it were true." He replaced the photo of her and Haley at the water park. "Elloree is driving Mom a little crazy, a bit too energetic. Would you mind sharing what preschool Haley goes to?"

The kettle whistled, and Tiffany poured. "I'm trying to think if Emma has ever said anything about being happy with the place or not. I guess yes because Haley's been there awhile."

They could be strangers—maybe were, given the years that had passed. Still, she was comfortable with the safe topics and swirled honey in her tea with a jolt of happiness. The spoon clattered at the direction her thoughts were heading. "I'll write the details down as soon as I hand you this coffee."

"Thanks," he said from only a few feet away. She'd been so intent on the task at hand that she'd not heard him approach. "I'll take that. Can we sit on the couch?"

"Um, sure." Her heart stuttered. He obviously had more on his mind than Elloree's daycare situation. She pulled a saucer out of the cabinet for her tea. She never bothered and wasn't trying to impress him, but she knew she'd spill, and she did, only a few steps forward. Her hand trembled like her mother's after years of anxiety.

Nick took one gulp and then found the coaster on the end table and gingerly placed his cup on it. He leaned forward, the fingers of his right hand twisting his wedding ring. "My wife's dead."

Tiffany choked on her tea and almost dropped the mug on the way to putting it on the bare coffee table. "I'm sorry."

He pinched the bridge of his nose, shaking his head. "No, I'm sorry. I couldn't have worded that more badly if I tried. I just wanted to clear the air. I keep seeing you looking, wondering what we're doing here."

"So, the ring?" She'd almost said "I'm sorry" again, so these substitute words erupted, harsh. "I mean—"

He tugged. The ring must not have come off for a long time.

"Don't." That one word was softer. "Not on my account, not because I brought it up. When you're ready."

For the first time, his gaze locked with hers. "Some would say I should have been ready a long time ago. We weren't even married that long." His shoulders dropped, and the hollows of his cheeks deepened.

If he cried… Tiffany shivered. The last time she'd seen him cry was at the courthouse when his parents fought over custody of him. Not during the trial, where strangers could see, but back at her house when he came to see her that night after it was all over.

"It doesn't matter how long you were married. You lost someone you loved."

"Yeah." He drew in a deep breath. "I didn't say anything in Sunday school because it's always so awkward. Tell people that you're a widower, and you get lots of sympathy and lots of casseroles. I didn't want either. And Sunday night, well, you were worried about your sister, and I needed to do my job. It would have been out of place to just drop it in there. But"—he held up empty hands, palms up—"I couldn't keep talking to you without you knowing, couldn't show up Saturday."

Tiffany struggled to keep up. She wondered what a friend, without their history, would say. "How did you meet?"

His grin was weak. "In the Marines. We married because of Elloree. I'm not proud of the fact, but we were two marines in a bad place who'd both lost people we thought we were going to marry."

She came this close to saying that he'd left her, so why had he needed to turn to someone else? She forced herself to remain quiet, mute in the face of grief.

"Then, she found out she was pregnant. I asked her to marry me, not so much because it was the right thing to do, which it was, but because I wasn't going to have my child going through life without a father."

Of course, he wouldn't. His father had left him completely when he didn't get custody. All or nothing.

"We were happy, on the way to loving each other." The words kept coming, as if a gate had been unlocked. "Then, she died right after childbirth. I thought modern medicine had done away with the risk. Turns out, women still die in childbirth every day, even big, bad marines." His voice broke, and he almost gouged his eyes with rubbing them so hard.

Tiffany found herself on the couch, next to him, pulling his head down to her shoulder. If he'd resisted, the feat would have been impossible, but he clung.

Maybe a minute passed with them holding each other, their first real contact in the better part of a decade.

Nick sat up and put some distance between them. "I had no clue I'd fall apart like that. It's been years." One strand of hair was wet, but other than that, he could now be talking about the weather. "I guess there's a lot of guilt. Toward Lynna, for not loving her the way I should have. Toward you, for moving on the way I did."

She nodded, as if she understood.

He gave a shaky laugh. "So, how was your day?"

"Fine." She flinched at the abrupt switch but went with it. "Except Haley is about to drive me over the edge. I'd only just gotten her to bed when you called. We'd had three arguments and one time-out this evening alone."

Without warning, Nick reached an arm across her body. When she jerked away, he lifted one dark eyebrow. "Just need my coffee. So, Haley's taking out her anger with her mother on you, the custodial parent as of now? Wouldn't know anything about that."

"Elloree?" she asked, then caught herself. "No, she never knew her mother, did she? You. I remember you giving your mom so much grief."

"Yeah." He glanced away, his jawline ticking. "Lynna never even got to hold Elloree, so she has no memories of her mom. It was an emergency C-section, cord around Elloree's neck. When they got her out, the staff whisked her off. She was blue. Lynna had a reaction to the epidural they gave her. It was so fast."

Tiffany reached to take the coffee before he spilled on his uniform. "Had you told anyone the details before—before now?"

Where before, the emotion showed on his face like a sign, he now wore his masculine mask, stone-cold blank. "Yeah, her parents. Right after but not again, not since."

The still-hot coffee burned her fingers, but chills raced through the rest of her. He'd not told anyone between them and her. "Thank you, for telling me now." She moved back to the love seat.

He leaned over his knees for a few minutes and then looked up, calmer. "So, how was your day at school?"

Her tea sat cooling, the smell soothing. "I've actually been having a rough year so far. There's this one little boy, Sammy. We actually went to high school with his mother. Well, he failed last year because he wouldn't do anything. This morning, he didn't like what we had for breakfast and sat down on the floor and refused to move."

Her voice became a droning in her brain, but it felt so good to have somebody listen. His dark eyes watched her, followed her when she took a sip of the tepid tea, and she felt more warmed by that gaze than what little heat trickled down her throat.

They talked about nothing more serious than what cereal bar she'd have on hand so her problem student would eat rather than stage a coup, until Nick upended his empty coffee cup.

"I think that's my sign." He pushed himself to his feet. "And last I checked, it's a school night. Enjoy that casserole, and see you on Saturday?"

The question had her confused for a second. "Yes, I'm looking forward to it. Oh, let me write down Haley's daycare information."

She grabbed both their cups, took a detour to her desk, and set them down long enough to scrawl the name and address on a scrap of paper. "Here. They'd love to be in the same class."

He stood next to her, bringing with him a new sense of discomfort. Knowing that he wasn't married, that there could be something between them if they so chose, made her more aware of him and the depth of the feelings that had seemingly gone nowhere in seven long years.

She hurried to hand him the note. "Here. Thank your mom for me."

"I will." He flipped the note over and grinned for the first time that night. "Are you sure you don't need this appointment card?"

Tiffany swiped it out of his hand. "Oh, good grief. Here."

Once again, he knew her too well.

If she smiled any bigger, she'd start to cry.

CHAPTER 10

FRIDAY WAS THE LAST DAY of classes before Christmas break, and her first-grade babies were excited and rambunctious. She anticipated Saturday night way more than she should. Wondering about Emma, where she was and when she'd return, got pushed into the background, except when Haley interrogated her again. Tiffany had started reading her devotional every morning for the first time in years, and she found some peace. Until somebody proved otherwise, she would believe that her sister was coming back as she'd promised, and she was out there somewhere with a man she met on the internet. It wasn't as if her sister hadn't been stupid where men were concerned before.

For Haley's sake, she needed to put on a smile and wear the armor of the Lord.

Saturday, Nick arrived ten minutes early, which was okay because she'd been ready for half an hour. She firmly bought into the saying "Early is good, and on time is late." Of course, she'd had the whole day to drive herself crazy with trying to choose an outfit for what was ostensibly a playdate.

Haley stuck to her side like a barnacle. It was as if she had a toddler rather than her big girl. She hadn't asked about her mother in twenty-four hours, and Tiffany hated herself, but she was relieved. She didn't know what to tell her anymore, didn't understand how her sister had called one time and then not called again. They needed to know something, or they would both be the size of beach balls by Christmas. The amount of comfort food available to them in the South was scary.

She opened the door. Nick stood there, olive-green fleece bringing out his dark eyes, with Elloree in his arms. The little girl wore a beautiful, impractical white coat with snowy mittens and a floppy hat. She looked like a snow princess in a place where it rarely snowed. Haley poked her head through the open space between Tiffany's body and the doorframe and grinned at their visitors.

Tiffany had dressed her niece in all red to match her own red jacket. Going all red would have been too vivid, so Tiffany toned down the rest of her outfit with black leggings and boots. Green would have been a good choice, too, but white washed her out like yellow ink on a sheet of printer paper. Haley's blond hair against the red jacket shone like the different shades of fire, red and yellow. The child's blue eyes gleamed like the hottest part of the flame.

"You ready?" Nick's eyes swept over her, and there was an appreciation there that she'd missed. A lot. She'd attended college, and she'd dated, but no other guy had looked at her just like that. "I thought we'd grab some barbecue on the way."

"Yeah?" Tiffany remembered their long-lasting feud over the best barbecue in town. "There are some new players in town, since..." She hesitated. Somehow, they'd avoided talking about their past, even in passing.

"I know." Nick met her eyes with a steady gaze. "And some of our favorites are gone, but that's all right. Things change."

If those words didn't drip with hidden meaning, it never rained in Charleston.

"I want macaroni and cheese, Daddy," Elloree said, and Tiffany put the past away on the shelf where it had been waiting for so long. It would still be there later, when they were ready to unearth it for inspection. It might sneak up on them, but their memories definitely lingered.

"Gotcha." Nick swiped his daughter's hand and interlaced their fingers. Tiffany almost got caught up in times that she'd held hands with the man, but she had a little girl poking her head out the door.

"Haley, wait. I need to get my purse." She disconnected herself from the little huddle at her door and rushed around the apartment, grabbing her keys, purse, and gloves. There was no snow, but there was a biting wind coming in from the shore.

"I thought we'd take my car. I can just transfer Haley's car seat." Nick had entered behind her and stood just inside the threshold.

She sucked in a breath at the thought that he was in her home, back in her life. She didn't know whether she should even be friends with this man. She'd been so badly hurt before. "Um, yes. That sounds like a good idea. My car is pretty small. What do you drive?"

They walked out into the stairwell, and her heart rate settled down. Nick really didn't need to answer her as they herded little girls in the direction of the parking lot and the extended-cab pickup parked in a visitor's spot. Tiffany unlocked her little car, and they made the shift. Nick had the hateful job of figuring out the car seats while she held on to two squirming little monkeys.

"Elloree." His voice came across the few feet separating them, stern and just harsh enough to produce results. Both little girls stopped.

"He's scarier than Mama," Haley whispered in one of those too-loud stage whispers.

"He's a daddy," Elloree said, not moving an inch.

"Okay. In you go, Haley girl." With their better behavior, his voice went back to lighthearted and easy.

Haley hurried to obey and chatted to the man as if she didn't know when she'd see one of this alien species again. "Aunt Tiffy calls me Haley bug. Mama calls me Haley boo. What do you call Elloree?"

"Elloree." Nick kept up the serious daddy voice, but he grinned like a Cheshire cat. "That's her name, isn't it?"

Elloree had either built up more armor, or she knew she had her daddy wrapped around her little finger as long as she behaved. "He calls me sweet cheeks, don't you, Daddy?"

Tiffany started around the car, but Nick yelled for her to stop.

"What?" She looked at the pavement as if there might be glass or—in a different season around here—an alligator.

"Wait. I'm supposed to open your door for you!" He practically ran around the truck. "Don't go making me look bad in front of the little girls. I'm their role model for how a man should act, you know."

Tiffany's fingers stretched for the door handle, but she hesitated, her fatal flaw. She should have acted without dithering; she should have been faster. "This is a playdate."

His surprised expression captured her complete attention for a few seconds. Then, something clicked behind those intelligent brown eyes. "Yes, it is. It's a play*date*. Am I right, girls?"

The girls shouted their agreement.

She slid into the passenger seat without offering any more resistance. He walked around the front of the car, the wind whipping his jacket open and shut. Silence reigned as he backed out of the parking spot and headed for Highway 78.

The girls chatted away in the back seat, mostly about what they would eat and what the lights would look like. As far as Tiffany knew, Haley had never been, but she talked about Christmas things like Santa and Rudolph as if she had gone a thousand times.

Their childish voices gave the adults the perfect cover for what passed as a private conversation.

"So, I'm thinking we start filling in some holes here." Nick's truck had the fancy screen in the middle of the console with the map of the area. She'd lived in the area her whole life. She could have given him directions, but he didn't ask. "How about you catch me up on Tiffany. What have you been doing with yourself since high school?"

The wording was so careful she almost laughed. She must have communicated her unease, because his hands tightened on the steering wheel. His white knuckles gave her pause. If they were going to even approach being friends or at least get the girls together without giving them the opposite of good role models, her heart needed to change, and it needed to change right now.

She focused on the trees going by, mostly bare of leaves with the occasional pine or live oak. "After you left"—her pride at saying those words without rancor knew no bounds—"I worked at the pet store for the summer."

"You always did love animals." He merged onto the highway.

Tiffany didn't have to work on her heart change when fluffy animals were at stake. "Did you see my rabbit?"

"You have a rabbit?" Elloree squealed from the back seat. If they'd thought their conversation was in the least private, they would have been sorely mistaken. "I want to see!"

"Yes, his name is Bunny Foo Foo." Haley sang the name. It was impossible to say her bunny's name without singing the stupid song. Sometimes, Tiffany regretted the name choice, but then again, her niece looked adorable in the rearview mirror.

"Wow, Tiff. You just had to go there," Nick complained, but he was laughing. "Can we see the bunny when we get back?"

"Yes." She laughed, knowing full well that both girls would be sleeping rag dolls by the time they get back. "And if it's too late, maybe some other time."

Nick's hands were loose on the wheel. It was the rest of his body that stilled. "Will there be a next time?"

Tiffany relaxed her own hands in her lap, just in case he was as aware of her as she was of him. "The girls seem to have hit it off. I think we can be civil to each other for their sake."

"Just civil?" He passed a small hybrid car with ease. "I think we'd moved past civil Wednesday night. So, about that next time, how about if it's just the two of us?"

"Without us?" Elloree whined. "That's not fair."

"Tell you what." Nick sounded like his patience with being interrupted might be wearing a bit thin. "Why don't you two watch a movie for a little bit?"

Tiffany hadn't noticed the screen protruding from the ceiling right between the two front seats.

"Movie, movie," the girls started chanting.

Nick pushed some buttons, his eyes never leaving the road. "How about The Bible Chronicles?"

"Yay!" Elloree cheered alone. Haley clearly didn't recognize the title, and Tiffany's face burned.

"Haley's never seen the series. When she's at my house, we don't watch television." She left unsaid the fact that Emma had long ago abandoned her faith, hence the need for Tiffany to take her niece to all church-related events. "So, it will be a new adventure."

"Yay!" Haley was a few minutes late.

"Okay," Nick said in his regular guy voice. "Now that the screen rules supreme, let's back it up to before Bunny Foo Foo. Did you end up at Lowcountry University as planned?"

It was so strange to think that her ex–closest friend knew so little about her now. "You already knew I'd been accepted. I lived at home because my scholarships only covered tuition and related costs. They didn't cover room and board. I majored in elementary education and loved it. I worked on the weekends at Burger Shack to pay for my car."

"Did you get to do any of the typical college stuff? Parties, football?"

She ran a finger along the edge of the window, the cold outside air seeping through, invigorating rather than uncomfortable. "I never was one for parties, but I did attend some football games." She smiled. "You got extra credit if you helped sell concessions."

His brow furrowed, evidence of his concern that she hadn't been able to enjoy life while constantly working.

"Don't worry. My sisters and I did things. Valerie and I had movie nights and popcorn. We went to the beach. I've got good friends and my church. I'm teaching first-graders at Azalea Elementary, and I love my babies. I love teaching."

He drummed his thumbs against the steering wheel. "So, did you meet anyone special?"

Some mean part of her reared its ugly head and wanted nothing more than to make him squirm. But, at some point in these last years, she'd grown up. So, instead, she decided to tell him the simple truth. "I dated, but no one seemed to stick. That's okay. I'm single, and I'm happy with that."

He swerved, not enough to cross the dotted lines separating the three lanes of traffic but enough to have her wondering at his reaction. She hadn't meant she wasn't open to a relationship, even though she had been content before he held that door open on Sunday.

Now, she wasn't so sure she was content.

Nick's tight grip on the steering wheel might just indicate he wasn't content, either.

CHAPTER 11

THEY PULLED INTO THE OLD-FASHIONED restaurant's parking lot. The Palmetto Pig was one of the few Mauldin's restaurants still operating. A whole family of brothers had built barbecue restaurants in the Charleston area and even up into Columbia, in competition to the point of a family feud.

As far as she was concerned, the public had only benefited from their squabbles. She loved a different item at each of the restaurants. One of the local places' onion rings were the size of saucers. The place in Columbia had mustard-based sauce that lingered on the palate and could be ordered online. Palmetto Pig had vegetable sides that couldn't be beat.

"Do they have macaroni and cheese here, Daddy?" Elloree was nothing if not consistent.

"She's never been?" Tiffany asked. "What kind of daddy are you?"

Nick swung Haley out of her car seat and deposited her next to her aunt. "The kind that's only been back in South Carolina for a few weeks. Before that, we bounced from base to base like good grunts, and then, I was at the police academy."

It was on the tip of her tongue to ask, but she shied away from anything else serious. This was supposed to be a fun night for the girls, especially Haley, to take her mind off the fact that her mother was missing. "Well, now that you're here…"

"She will dutifully be introduced to all things southern, starting with serious macaroni and cheese and barbecue." He had his daughter's hand in his, and they swung their arms in a long arc. "So, to answer your question, Elle, yes. They have the best mac and cheese ever."

"I want fried okra, Aunt Tiffy," Haley said. Tiffany gave Nick a self-satisfied nod. Yes, that's right. Her niece asked for okra.

He held the door for the three of them, and they were seated pretty quickly for a Saturday night. They all ordered the buffet. The girls talked about the show they'd been watching, and they talked about Haley's preschool. They talked until Nick ordered them to eat. Tiffany thanked the Lord. She needed some lighthearted right about now. The warmth of pulled pork and creamy macaroni and cheese in her belly helped the mellow mood, and she felt a different kind of peace. It was good to just enjoy being with people she liked.

Eventually, she surrendered. Her eyes were often bigger than her stomach. "I'm done."

Nick stood without saying a word and was back in a few minutes with to-go boxes. "Here you go. I don't know about you, but we live off of leftovers. Since my cooking skills are pretty much limited to things that come out of a box with very specific instructions."

Tiffany spooned sweet-potato casserole into a protected side slot. In some ways, she felt like she was getting to know an unknown quantity in Nick. Seven years, particularly at their age, meant so many changes. "I've gotten to be a pretty good cook, living on my own these last few years. Plus, Granny Linda taught me a lot when I was growing up."

"How is she?" He must have been able to interpret the answer by the way her permanent-around-him smile evaporated. "Oh, I'm sorry. When?"

Time had healed that wound to some degree, since she was confident the sweet old lady who'd taught her so much while her mother worked two jobs and dated an endless string of strange men had gone to the right place after she passed. "When I was a senior in college. She had a stroke and then fell. It was one of those times when everybody says it's a blessing."

"But it doesn't mean you don't miss her." He had this way of focusing on her that said she was the only woman in the world right then, maybe ever. Seven years might be a long time as far as the living they'd done, but it was the blink of an eye as far as how she felt about him.

"No, no, it doesn't." Her gaze fell, and she stared at his ring. Now that she knew he was a widower, she could only guess at his own sense of loss. "Haley, let's go to the restroom before we drive to the park."

Nick glanced up from his daughter's leftover mac and cheese and fries. The man had a wide-eyed hopeful look. "Would you take Elloree, too? I can't tell you how hard it is with a little girl her age and the men's bathroom."

She blinked. "Of course. Wow, I never thought."

The waitress appeared with their check. Tiffany made a determined effort to hand the woman her credit card, but Nick shooed her away.

"I've got this." He lifted one dark eyebrow. "Role model, Tiffany, role model."

She gave her sigh extra volume and grabbed two little girls' hands. He continually sent signals that this was a date. Friends paid their own way. The evening had been a bad idea.

"I'm having so much fun." Haley leaned into her side. Haley's little head bumped against her, and Tiffany absorbed the impact like a hug. This evening wasn't about her, and she needed to relax. Nick had invited them, so he might see himself as the host and feel it was his obligation to pay under those circumstances.

"Me, too!" Elloree jumped up and down, straining at the bit.

The girls talked all the way through going to the bathroom, washing their hands, and heading back to the table. Tiffany could predict a headache by the evening's end, but it would be, oh, so worth it, knowing Haley had gone for several hours without asking about her mother.

Nick had gotten them refills on their drinks in to-go cups, as well. She could get used to helping hands like this. She shook herself mentally and held out the little girls' hands. "All washed up and ready for our next adventure, sir."

The man's smile could power a whole street of Christmas lights. "I can't wait. Here are some drinks for the road. You know, they don't do that everywhere in the country. I had no idea until I left the South, but out west, they don't do to-go cups."

Tiffany had never traveled farther from home than two states away in any direction, which meant she'd never left the southern United States. "I had no idea. That's a shame, because this woman is always thirsty."

"I remembered." His smile powered down to the "I know you like the back of my hand" grin.

She couldn't respond without bringing up skeletons better left in the grave, so she gave him what she hoped was a vague smile and not a grimace. She wrapped Haley in her jacket and handed her the small cup of sweet tea. The drink wasn't much better than soda, but it was a rare treat and could probably explain the bouncing up and down on her tippy toes.

"Settle down, Haley." The words demanded obedience, but she laughed while she said it, so the effectiveness left a lot to be desired. "Or I won't let you have sweet tea again."

"No, Aunt Tiffy." The little girl's heels thumped to the floor. "I'll be good. I promise."

Nick shepherded them to the door and chuckled. "That's a new discipline technique. The sweet tea timeout."

They all giggled and piled into the truck. The movie started again, and Nick and Tiffany were left with the conversation they started earlier. Tiffany couldn't see talking about herself anymore, not with so many unanswered questions about his life after he drove off to basic training.

"It's your turn," she said, knowing she sounded like her old timid self. "What happened to you after you left town to be a big, bad marine?"

Her wording left a lot to be desired. He threw her one of those looks that said he wanted to say something but was holding back. She could be reading too much into a simple expression, but there it was. She had no idea why she was the recipient, since he'd been the one to leave her behind.

"I became a big, bad marine." At first, it seemed he was going to leave it at that.

If he'd seen combat, she didn't want to pry. If he'd been injured, she would have heard through the high school gossip around town. Then again, she hadn't heard anything about his marriage, and none of their mutual friends had attended the ceremony as far as she knew. On the other hand, they might not have wanted to mention his name around her given how desolate she'd been those first few months. She'd withdrawn and lost contact with a number of people because all she'd had the energy for was working, eating, and sleeping—and not enough of those last two.

"Sorry." Nick's profile stood out against the darkness that had fallen while they ate. His cheekbones had grown more pronounced in the intervening years. Everything about him was a man and not the boy who'd left. "That's not fair. You didn't hold back on me. It was tough. What can I say with two little girls with big ears sitting in the back seat?"

"We don't have big ears," Elloree said. "Do we, Daddy? You're just joking."

Nick gave a short laugh, and his very straight teeth—he'd had braces in high school, and she'd still thought he was cute—gleamed in the headlights of passing cars. "No, baby girl, you don't have big ears. They're perfect little seashell ears, just like the rest of you."

Elloree set off on a giggling fit, and after a few seconds of confusion, Haley joined her. Tiffany had never seen her niece laugh so hard. Maybe even before Emma disappeared, things might not have been going so well. She'd been so busy she hadn't realized.

"So, I made it through Parris Island, barely. With just my mom at home for so long, I really hadn't been disciplined much."

"You were in good shape, though." And wasn't that a strange thing for a woman on a playdate to say?

Nick turned toward her long enough to give her a drive-by grin. "Yeah, I was, but mentally, I was a weakling. I'm not ashamed to say that the Marines toughened me up in a good way. They were harsh, but I needed harsh. When I was stationed in Iraq, I was very glad that they'd been brutal, because war is brutal."

They joined the line to enter the county park. Tiffany dug in her purse and pulled out cash for the entrance fee. "Nick, you have to let me pay. There's more than one kind of role model. Friends do their part, right, Haley?"

"Yes, ma'am." The little girl sounded distracted, maybe because she was engrossed in a song about a sling and a rock and a giant.

Nick snickered and held out his hand for the money. "Far be it from me to teach the girls to be selfish. Thank you."

"You're welcome." Tiffany sat back in her seat, satisfied for the moment.

A county employee gestured with a flashlight, and they followed the traffic to the right. Nick shut down the movie, and the girls didn't complain more than expected given they were being asked to switch gears mid-movie. The Christmas lights caught their attention and didn't let go.

With corporate sponsors and thousands of volunteer hours and over two million lights, the Christmas Carnival was billed as Charleston's favorite holiday attraction. Tiffany had researched it earlier in the week so she could explain to Haley what they would be doing. The fact that Tiffany had never been was just another sad item on her childhood list. It also meant she oohed and aahed with the girls as if she were their age.

Elloree pointed. "There's a dinosaur."

"That's a pterodactyl." Nick drove with the traffic, which meant roughly five miles per hour so they could see every Christmas and nursery-rhyme character.

When they reached the fork in the road, he gave Tiffany the choice. "I thought we'd stop and maybe buy some s'mores, walk the Enchanted Trail. Or we can keep driving."

CHAPTER 12

TIFFANY'S MIND WENT BACK AND forth like a pendulum. Stopping meant more time, so very close to being alone with him. The girls were already buzzing on sweet tea; they didn't need any more sugar. There were so many good reasons to cut this evening short, not the least of which was the parts of their past they hadn't bothered to mention. Maybe some things were meant to stay buried.

Each decision seemed to either lead to more of a relationship with this man, or not.

"Tiffany?" He was on the verge of holding up the line.

"Oh, who am I kidding? You had me at chocolate."

"Thought so." His smirk could be wiped off his face at any moment, or he could end up paying for their s'mores and be broke by the end of the evening.

Never mind the girls, who had to be physically restrained from running off to see the next thing and the next thing, Tiffany had one of the best nights of her life. They roasted marshmallows over the firepit. At one point, Nick's stick caught on fire, and he puffed out his cheeks, trying to extinguish the flame. The girls thought it was one of the funniest things they'd ever seen, and they laughed so hard Tiffany took their graham crackers away so no food would be sacrificed in the name of humor.

There was a sand sculpture done by adults who had to be artists in their real lives. There was other artwork done by schoolchildren.

The Enchanted Trail was just a walk through the woods with more lights, but it was dark. The girls held hands, which left the adults by themselves, a few feet behind for safety's sake but still almost alone.

"Do you remember that time at Dorchester Hall for Fright night?"

Dorchester Hall was a historic plantation that put on one horrifying Halloween trail every year. For the life of her, Tiffany couldn't remember why she'd ever consented to go. "Did you talk me into that? Because I'm the last person who should go to a haunted house, much less a terrifying trail through the woods."

"Still?" he said, his grin visible in the glow from the lights. "No, there was a whole group going, and we didn't want to be left out, which was stupid now that I think about it."

She concentrated on a display of the three wise men off in the distance. "I was scared for weeks. I can remember being terrified when the people from church came caroling at my grandmother's, because I didn't know what the sound was at first."

"That didn't stop y'all from letting us in and feeding us pecan-pie cookies."

He remembered a lot of details from back then, almost as if he'd cared. If he'd cared so much, why had he left without a backward glance?

"Are you staying at your mama's house?" she asked, because he'd skipped a lot in his too-short story as to what he'd been doing these last few years.

"Yes." They were walking so close to each other on the narrow trail that he brushed against her arm. "I found I just can't work the hours I do and take care of Elloree the way she needs to be taken care of. For a long time, I had help from one of my buddies' wives, but that ended when they moved."

He didn't mention how hard it had been to raise a baby without Lynna, but her absence had clearly left a big hole in their lives. "Why did you quit the Marines?"

"Same reason. Elloree needed a parent who was home. I was going to be deployed again if I re-upped, and she would have ended up with my mother anyway. I'd rather be part of her life than not."

He was a good father and loved his daughter very much. He'd served his country and seen things she could only imagine. None of this fit with a man who would just walk out on the girl he'd sworn he loved.

Tiffany tripped over a tree root.

She would have fallen flat on her nose if Nick's lightning-fast reflexes—she couldn't understand how he moved so fast—hadn't stopped her descent.

He stood there for much longer than was needed to get her back on her feet. Both his hands encircled her upper arms, the warmth of his touch permeating the thick fabric of her jacket. Slowly, she lifted her gaze to meet his. "Thank you. I'm still a klutz."

"You never were a klutz," he contradicted her. "You always give the conversation or whatever you're doing everything you've got. When you focus, you are all grace."

Tiffany fought the urge to melt against him in response to those, oh, so sweet words. She needed to remember how devastated she'd been when he left. The trail ended, and they reached the parking lot. The conversation had to end, too, because cars moved in and out and the girls seemed oblivious to danger, as was to be expected of children their age.

Tiffany grabbed Haley from behind. "Boo," she said, trying to make being grabbed fun.

Haley jumped like she'd sprouted short-range wings. "Aargh."

Elloree squealed. The girl acted nothing like the progeny of two hardened marines. "Daddy."

He scooped her up but then held her still. "I'm not stupid, so why did I just do that? Tossing a girl who's eaten her fill of barbecue and macaroni and cheese and—"

"Some mores!" She mangled the words, but boy, did she shine.

"—is not a good idea."

The girls made it through the rest of the lights, but then, they were out. Haley was doing the head-bobbing thing, and it was almost a craving to reach back there and support her before something snapped. Elloree's chin jutted, pushing her head back so she slept without bobbing but with her mouth wide open. Tiffany's grandmother would have warned the child she was going to catch flies like a Venus flytrap if she didn't watch out. Of course, warning a slumbering child about anything made no sense.

"Nick"—her voice took on a hushed quality—"if you don't mind, what made you become a police officer?"

The dark hid any physical reaction on his part, but there was a few seconds' hesitation. "I was assigned as an MP—military police—in Iraq. The war in Iraq was pretty much over by the time I shipped out and about as peaceful as this war gets. I was stationed at a big air base and saw no action whatsoever."

She thanked the good Lord for huge blessings.

"I guess you could say I felt some survivor's guilt. So many of my buddies were stationed at FOBs—

forward operating bases—and didn't make it back or made it back damaged. I had training in police work, and I felt I could do some good." He tapped the steering wheel with one thumb, a telltale sign of unspoken emotion.

"Thank you." Whether she thanked him for the answer or his service, she didn't know.

"Thank you for asking." He switched gears and turned into her apartment parking lot. "So many people think I'll freak out if they ask what happened. I want to talk about those years. It's not as if they never happened. Even if something bad happened to me, I'd want you to know about it."

Warmth spread through her body, and she ignored the source. He couldn't mean her in particular; he had to mean people in general. When he pulled into the same spot, still empty as if it had his name on it, she rotated her body slightly. "Thank you for a lovely night."

Maybe it was instinct or old memories that had never really died, but Nick leaned in for a kiss. Maybe she wanted it to happen, maybe her feelings had only hidden in a corner of her heart somewhere, but she almost let him.

"What?" She reared back, then muted her voice to a vicious whisper. "What are you doing?"

He'd parked under a streetlight, so she had a clear view of his face. He looked older than he was—and very hurt. "What do you mean what am I doing?

I think it would be pretty obvious I was going to kiss you. That's what normally happens at the end of a date."

"This was a playdate." She fumbled with the seat belt, which was defeating her. "Not a date date."

"Come on, Tiffany. We obviously both still have feelings for each other. Whatever happened in the past, we can work those things out."

"We can't work out." Tiffany was so flustered she now tripped over her words.

"What?" He reached over to unfasten the recalcitrant seat belt for her, his hands brushing her hip. "What can't we work out?" The shock at his touch must have shown on her face because he held up his hands in surrender. He waited.

"Nick." She felt as if she'd been tossed into the air after she'd indulged in too much of a pleasant evening. "You left. I didn't hear from you for seven years. You can't just come back and act like nothing happened."

He took his turn at leaning away from her. She could leave, but she waited.

After a few moments of a stare-down, he rubbed his face with his left hand. "I think it's late, and we're going to need time to talk this out, because I remember things very differently."

"Okay." Anger and whispering so much had her throat raw. "You're right. I don't want to talk about this right now."

He whipped off his seat belt and slammed open his door. "You never wanted to talk if it involved the possibility of conflict, Tiff."

She watched as he walked around the car, stunned silent.

Before she could come up with a response, he stood outside her door with his hand on the handle. She watched him take a deep breath and count to at least ten—maybe twenty since the situation required the extra cooldown. Then, he changed his mind and opened the back door instead.

"I'll carry Haley for you. I'm going to apologize for snapping at you, because obviously, we have a lot to work out. I'm sorry I tried to kiss you too soon. That's on me. But your unwillingness to talk about the hard stuff—that part's on you." He unbuckled the little bobbing body and cradled Haley's head to keep it from getting banged on the car door.

Tiffany said nothing, since she couldn't think of anything to say. She followed him meekly up the stairs and unlocked her apartment door. She made a move to take her niece, but he waved her off.

"I'll put her in her bed. Just show me the way."

Tiffany's chest constricted with the same unease she'd experienced earlier. Every step he took brought him further into her life.

When he'd tucked Haley into bed, he straightened and searched her eyes. "I'll see you at church tomorrow?"

She nodded.

He lifted his chin in acknowledgment and left.

She had to assume he'd closed the door behind him, because she couldn't find a way to move. Her body and her heart were both paralyzed by a crazy mix of emotions. Hope and shame.

Not a good way to end the night.

CHAPTER 13

SUNDAY MORNING LOOMED IN FRONT of Tiffany. Today wasn't just a regular day. The Christmas program was this morning, and Haley had won the coveted part of Mary. The script required this Mary only to speak two verses and to sit there and hold a baby doll in swaddling clothes. In all the practices, Haley beamed at the right times and rode on the backs of some bigger boys—aka the donkey—at the right time. She was a star.

Tiffany had no idea whether the little girl could play the part without her mother in the audience. Tiffany didn't even know whether she could bear to watch without Emma there. The fact that she still hadn't returned or called again after all this time made no sense.

The morning dragged on, and then, it was time. They held the program during the second service. It meant no Sunday school hour, but it was the best way to get the most people in attendance. And after last night, Tiffany could only be glad there would be no chance of a discussion hour. She didn't know whether she could face Nick any more than she could face the Christmas program all by her lonesome.

The music started, and she flipped open the program.

Nick took the empty seat next to her. "Is this okay?" he whispered.

The shock almost had her jumping, in church, on the third row, where everybody behind them could see her reaction. Somehow, he seemed to have recovered from what happened last night. He also looked way too good in a long-sleeved polo shirt and khakis.

What could she say? "Of course."

He narrowed those big brown eyes at her, but he didn't say anything more. For one thing, they were in serious danger of being shushed.

She picked up her cell phone and recorded the procession into the sanctuary. This was one of the rare times it was considered okay to take pictures in the holy place. She wouldn't do this for long. She wanted to focus on the program itself, but Emma was out there somewhere, missing one of her daughter's firsts.

Haley rode in on the back of a middle school boy. The boy, Adam Riordan, wore a gray sweatshirt and sweatpants and had some fake ears large enough to be bunny ears. Haley wore a pale blue scarf tied around her head with only wisps of her blond hair poking out. Her dress was a darker blue, and her little feet swung off the side of the donkey's back. She held the collar of Adam's shirt with one hand and her plump belly with the other. The padding shifted from side to side in a strange, adorable pattern.

Sporting angel wings, Elloree danced up the aisle. The crowd gently laughed at the little girl pirouetting up to the altar.

Nick pinched the bridge of his nose, trying to squelch either laughter or humiliation. She hoped it was the former. His little girl lit up the makeshift stage.

A six-year-old Joseph helped Haley dismount from her steed and led her to the stable. She picked up the baby doll Jesus and cradled him to her chest. The look of love and tender care on the little girl's face hurt Tiffany's heart.

Nick reached over and squeezed her arm in what had to be a gesture of comfort, and she gave him a watery smile. He turned back toward the front, and she forced herself not to think about the night before or his presence next to her. The shepherds were glaring at the angels, who couldn't stand still, but they all belted out the words.

"I can't believe she learned the songs so fast," she whispered. Elloree was a ham. A slightly older girl, who happened to be the one standing in front of the microphone, yelled the words. Elloree gave her the side-eye as Clara—that was the older girl's name—overpowered everyone else. One of the boys mouthed every other word, and the other little ones were barely audible, so it really came down to Elloree and Clara. Then, on the last line, Elloree leaned forward and pushed her way to the microphone, effectively getting the last word.

Clara crossed her arms, none too happy, and Elloree grinned. The audience surrendered all dignity and burst out laughing. Elloree soaked it up.

"Good Lord, what have I created?" Nick groaned and laughed at the same time, an interesting combination.

The two women in charge of the program ushered the younger children off the stage, and the middle schoolers stepped up to read the next Bible passage.

Haley didn't budge from holding the baby doll, her face serious. When it came her time to stand and say her verses, she placed the make-believe Jesus down as carefully as if he were real. She walked—she didn't run or skip—to the microphone and folded her hands in front of her waist. "How can this be, when I am a virgin?"

A tall girl playing the part of Gabriel answered.

Tiffany held her breath. She and Haley had practiced all week.

"I am the Lord's servant." Her niece didn't waver. "May it be with me as you have said."

The purity of the words said in the little girl's voice—a little girl who missed her mama so much—

had tears rolling down Tiffany's face. No matter what, she didn't let the hand holding her phone shake. She would never forget what it felt like to see faith embodied in a child.

Haley broke character just long enough to smile in Tiffany's direction. She sniffled and smiled back. Nick produced a handkerchief from somewhere. Did men even carry them anymore?

"Thank you." She blew her nose without thinking, and horror crept through her chest. "Oh," she whispered, looking at him, unable to remove the soiled cloth. "I'm so sorry."

He winked. "That's what it's for. You can wash it and return it on Wednesday."

She wanted to ask what was happening Wednesday, but the Christmas story continued to unfold in front of them. Her phone blinked. It was running out of charge. Haley's part was pretty much done, so she powered the device off and just enjoyed the show. There was the teenage boy who'd been too cool to attend Sunday school for the past year, who came out and played the part of Herod like a boss. Two high school girls did a duet that she would regret being unable to record. Their voices blended in a way that awed her.

Seven years had passed since that had been her up there, a shy second soprano, but everything had been right in the world back then.

The children processed out to the foyer, with the promise of being the first to have access to the cookies. Tiffany and Haley had made rice crispy treats in the shape of Christmas trees yesterday afternoon. It wasn't the most challenging recipe in the world, but finding a place for all the red and green sprinkles serving as decorations had kept the little girl occupied for an hour.

"Well, that was something." Nick towered over her. He'd bulked up a lot in addition to gaining a few inches since high school. "I'm thinking I need to enroll Elloree in dance classes or something." He rubbed his face as if the prospect terrified him.

Despite everything, Tiffany smiled. "I can see it now. In about one year, you'll be sewing ruffles on her tutu the night before the big recital."

If a man's eyes could bug out of his head and his face lose all color, Nick's did. "Woman. Are you trying to kill me?"

Tiffany laughed and shook her head. "No, just enjoying. Shall we go get our sugar fix?"

"Please." He grumbled as they made their way down the aisle. "So, before we see the girls, just in case you have plans. I don't want to get Elloree excited if the answer is no. Anyway, I have Wednesday off and thought we might go see the Christmas trees on Main Street."

A wave of sorrow that they continued to make plans without Emma came and went. Emma would be back, and Tiffany could still babysit Haley. "That would be nice."

"Great."

She could see him mentally checking one more item off his list. She'd always liked the way he made plans and kept his life so organized, naturally, seemingly without effort, where she had to be careful or she'd lose every possession she owned.

"Do you remember when we decorated that tree with the youth group and the whole thing fell over?" Nick seemed to want to remember the past.

Walker Square, a grassy area in front of the historic shops in Summer Creek, held several dozen Christmas trees decorated by civic groups and various churches. For Halloween, they'd dressed scarecrows in attire representing the groups' missions. Year after year, half a dozen of the really involved kids did everything. That year, she and Nick had participated in everything. Cheap dates, he'd argued. "Yes, I remember" was all she said now.

They made their way through the receiving line of children, shaking everyone's hand and saying, "Good job."

When she reached Haley, the little girl dropped the serious expression she'd worn all day and jumped into Tiffany's arms. "Aunt Tiffy, we get to eat the cookies. Did you see all of them?"

"Yes, I did, and no, you can't eat all of them. You'll get sick."

"Try me."

Tiffany snorted with shock. Her sweet, well-behaved niece had just gotten sassy.

Nick leaned over and gestured with his chin. "Hey, I brought the good stuff, store bought."

Her grin faltered. Her sister was missing, and she was happy, even if for a minute. Or more. She'd enjoyed herself last night, and the program had warmed her aching chest. "I'll be sure to get the recipe."

The thought of what they must look like, laughing and—no getting around it—flirting, wiped the grin away. She turned to find a plate and focused on Haley. "I think you can handle four cookies."

"Because I'm four." Haley bought the rationale, hook, line, and sinker. Tiffany's spurt of pride in her mothering skills disappeared when she realized Haley was picking out the biggest cookies in the room.

"Hey, wait a minute."

She looked up and caught Nick laughing at her. It occurred to her that she hadn't laughed this much for years. Her facial muscles protested, but her heart, well, it didn't need the sugar overload that she had coming.

The plate she carried for her and Haley full, Tiffany made her way to the corner where Valerie stood. Her friend didn't have a child in the game, but she volunteered to help because that's who she was.

"Hey, how are you doing?" The concern in her friend's eyes almost had Tiffany crying again.

Haley and Elloree chatted a few feet away, mouths full of the chocolate-peanut-butter-cup cookies they'd both chosen as a starting point. It was a family addiction on Haley's side. Nick was talking to one of the elders about him joining the maintenance committee. Tiffany stared at the plate in her hand and couldn't think of putting food in her churning stomach. "I'd be wonderful if Emma would just come home."

Valerie gave her a quick hug. "Still haven't heard from her again?"

Tiffany switched hands. "Not since that first night. Yet life keeps moving on. We went to the Dewee's Island Christmas Carnival last night."

Valerie's gaze moved from her to Nick and the girls. "We?"

Heat crept up Tiffany's neck, and she dipped her head to hide the impending doom. "Yes, we. Nick came with Elloree and took us."

Valerie knew everything about their past. Travis and Valerie had been the double to more of Nick and Tiffany's dates than she could remember. Valerie had sat on the living-room floor when Tiffany curled up on the rug after he left. "Are you sure? I mean…"

"I don't know." Tiffany stuffed a pecan praline in her mouth and bought herself some time. "Just found out a few nights ago that he's a widower, need time to adjust."

"Oh." Valerie usually had a more extensive vocabulary. She sipped some of the ubiquitous citrus punch and left behind a lime-sherbet mustache. "Poor man. I noticed the wedding ring last week—was it just last week? But I thought maybe his wife couldn't make it here yet or maybe she was deployed."

Tiffany blinked several times. She didn't know the full story and wondered how much she should say. "She died when Elloree was born."

"Oh." Valerie lifted a hand to her chest. "Poor man. He's been raising that little girl all on his own."

Tiffany followed her friend's gaze to the man balancing an empty cup on Haley's head. Nick did not elicit pity. He'd been a hero for his country, and now, he was a hero for his daughter. "No. He's not poor. I mean, it's sad about his wife, but he's doing good things with his life."

"Of course, he is." Valerie gave her a side hug, and Tiffany went to collect her niece.

"See you on Wednesday?" Nick's eyes danced with the mischief he'd been making and sparked the embers of a fire she'd thought long doused.

"Yeah." She smiled and pushed aside the question as to why he'd forgiven her for last night and why he hadn't been her hero seven years ago. "We'll see you then."

"I'll text you with the details."

CHRISTMAS CONFUSION

She trusted him that far. Not much further.

CHAPTER 14

WHILE THEY DROVE TO HER apartment, Haley's head jerked back and forth as she fought the good fight and lost. She fell asleep so deep her thumb slipped out of her mouth and dangled over the side of her car seat. For a few seconds, Tiffany stared at the child in the rearview mirror. Her heart overflowed, and she didn't want this to be over.

Her biological clock was a-ticking. She wanted that. She wanted a daughter whose hair would be a shade more brown than blond and whose eyes might be brown. If her offspring could tan when she couldn't, that would be okay, but she longed for her own family, not a borrowed one.

She was winded by the time she managed to unbuckle the dead weight that was her niece, bully her out of the car seat, and struggle up the flight of stairs. Unlocking the door almost undid her, but she triumphed.

When Haley was safely ensconced in the guest bed, Tiffany had a choice. Either she could take advantage of the opportunity and crash, or she could get things done. Eventually, the break would end, and a new semester would begin. She needed to be ready.

Groaning, she dragged herself to the desk and the waiting laptop. She'd no more than logged in when her phone buzzed with a text. Mrs. Melanie asked for the video she'd made.

I'M GOING TO POST IT ONLINE. Tiffany messaged before she thought it through.

Mrs. Melanie: THANK YOU! YOU'RE SO SWEET. SEE YOU NEXT WEEK FOR THE CHURCH POTLUCK.

Tiffany read the words and supplied the southern accent. She owed Mrs. Melanie a lot. The Sunday school director had been instrumental in getting her a scholarship for college, and she wouldn't forget the help when her own mother had thought a college education was a waste of money. Real adults got jobs and moved out as soon as they were eighteen.

Tiffany: SEE YOU THEN. HAVE A WONDERFUL WEEK!

Mrs. Melanie: YOU, TOO!

The video was ready to be posted, but Tiffany hesitated over the caption. Haley wasn't her daughter, no matter how much she loved the little girl. Emma had never had problems with her posting pictures of their outings before, but somehow, this felt different. Emma wasn't around to give permission. Tiffany exhaled. Emma wasn't around, period, and she couldn't see any danger in posting a video of her niece playing Mary in a Christmas pageant.

Haley and the wonderful children of Grace Church, Christmas program. So proud.

She posted.

She yawned. A nap sounded so good.

At some point in the measly half-hour nap, Haley crawled in beside her. The weight of the child's arm across her nose made it impossible to stay asleep and breathe.

"Ouch." Tiffany scooted to the side of the bed and inched her way out, trying to slip out unnoticed.

It didn't work. "Aunt Tiffy. Where are you going?"

"To the bathroom." Even if Tiffany hadn't needed to go, she needed the break. She was putting herself in auntie time-out but wasn't going to inform her niece.

"Can I come, too?"

"No, sweetie." Hurt for her niece softened any aggravation she felt at the disruptions in her sleep and in her life. She loved the little girl so much. "But I'll be right back. You know where I am."

"Yes, ma'am." Haley almost disappeared beneath the down comforter.

When Tiffany emerged, Haley was waiting outside the door. Even when Tiffany headed toward the living room, the child followed her so closely she might as well have been tethered. Tiffany kept going and headed for the desk that had been calling her name earlier. She'd also left her phone there, to charge and to not disturb. As soon as she touched the case, the phone rang. It didn't vibrate; it rang.

"Tiffany?" Emma. "Where's Haley? I need to talk to her. I can't believe I forgot the Christmas program."

Tiffany couldn't find the words, but she put the phone on speaker. There was someone at her side who deserved to hear every word. The action also solved the problem of her having to speak to her sister. She couldn't, not yet.

"Mama!"

"Haley." Emma's voice sounded strained, as if she'd reach across the space between them, grab her daughter, and squeeze her and hold her if she could. "My baby. I saw you on the video. I'm so sorry I couldn't come."

"Mama?" Haley's little fingers bit into Tiffany's forearm, pinching little half moons. "Where are you? Why aren't you here?"

"What do you mean? Didn't Aunt Tiffany tell you that I called?" Emma sounded baffled.

Tiffany wanted to reach through the telephone wires that no longer existed in the age of cell phones and jerk a knot in her sister. "You called one time, and I couldn't hear the majority of what you were saying. What could I actually tell your daughter?"

"But I asked you."

"You asked me what?" Now, Tiffany found it hard to breathe. Could her sister be implying that this horror was somehow her fault? "As of last Friday, you asked me to pick up Haley the way you normally do on the weekends. For one weekend while you worked. But you didn't go to work, did you? Where did you go, Emma?" She stepped away from the phone. "Tell Haley why you aren't here. You owe her an explanation, not me."

Emma coughed. "I do." Her voice came out hoarse and raw. Tiffany had the ugly thought that her sister deserved to be upset.

They could have clicked on video. She could have asked to switch over, but she didn't. She needed the distance of only hearing and not seeing.

"I'm sorry. I should have called. I didn't mean for it to happen. We were just going to be gone for the weekend."

We? Who was we? Her sister hadn't told her anything about anyone. Tiffany felt doubly—make it quadruply—betrayed.

"Then, his car broke down, and we went past the time to pick up Haley while we waited for the tow truck. That's when I called. Then, they didn't have the parts to fix the car. We've been waiting all week for them to get the car fixed. I didn't know you'd be worried."

"Worried?" Tiffany spit out the word like it was a cuss word, and she didn't curse—or at least, not much. "Is that what you call it?"

"I was a coward. I know that now. I just kept telling myself that you knew I was okay, and that way, I didn't have to explain."

"Mama, when are you coming home? I miss my room and Jimbo! Where's Jimbo?" Haley's voice got louder with every question. She bent over the phone, hands on her hips.

"He's with me, sweetheart. I'll be home soon. The car is going to be ready in two days. I'll be home on Tuesday."

Tuesday. She'd be back on Tuesday. They had plans with Nick for Wednesday morning. Tiffany knew her reaction bordered on insanity, but she didn't want her sister coming home now. She'd stayed away this long; she could stay away for quite some time—the foreseeable future. Tiffany walked away from the phone a few steps, then back, approach and avoid.

"Tiffany, do you forgive me?"

"I'm going to have to call Mama."

Emma moaned. "You told her? I mean, of course, you told her."

"Yes." Tiffany didn't recognize the cold person talking through her mouth. "I called her last Sunday, before you called and we knew you were at least safe. Then, Monday morning, I told her the good news. Then, the rest of the week, when you didn't call again, we didn't know what to think. You've put us through a lot. Just so you know, I called the police Sunday night. Again, before you called. You didn't show up for work, and your car was sitting in its parking spot, so I couldn't even think you'd just taken off. I reported you as a missing person."

A male voice said something in the background, deep and comforting.

"Who is he?"

"Justin. Justin's back, and he wants us to be a family."

Haley's father, the boy who left Emma high and dry when he found out she was pregnant, was back. The term fit better when someone came back from a vacation or maybe a semester abroad, not almost four years of being a deadbeat dad.

"He brought me up to Fort Bragg to see where we'd be living."

Tiffany's legs gave out, and she took both her and Haley to the floor. Not only had her sister put her through this weeklong hell, but she'd brought her and her niece so close that taking her away would be like ripping a seam. There would be one huge hole left behind, no matter how often they'd visit or call.

"Tiffany, are you there?"

"Yes. Emma, what time will you be here on Tuesday?" Tiffany reached over and held Haley close, just as much to comfort herself as her niece.

Again, the male voice spoke, and now, Tiffany recognized the way he called her sister "baby girl," as if years hadn't passed and her sister hadn't grown up.

"We can be down there for lunchtime,"

"I was going to take Haley to the Christmas tree display on Wednesday." Tiffany really didn't recognize herself. In the past, she'd not fought so hard—make that at all—for what she wanted. What she wanted right now wasn't about Nick, exactly; it was that Haley had been with her and trusted her. She wasn't going to just drop her like a ball passed from one person to another. "I'd still like to do that."

"Okay." Emma spoke fast, as if maybe, if she did whatever Tiffany asked her as fast as possible, then everything would be forgiven.

Forgive was a mighty big word.

"Haley?" A ragged inhale and exhale punctuated Emma's voice. "Mama loves you."

"I love you, too, Mama." Haley tucked herself in Tiffany's lap. Her head leaned against Tiffany's chest. No matter the vulnerability in her actions, there wasn't the slightest pause in her letting her mother back in.

"Good night. I'll see you in two days, sweetheart. Love you."

"Good night, Mommy."

Tiffany ended the call. If she was being childish, so be it. The child in her arms clung to her, and Tiffany didn't care if she wasn't being Christian or even what Emma might feel on the other end.

She was just numb—and done.

CHAPTER 15

SOMEONE MIGHT HAVE FOUND THEM there, in a heap on the floor, days later if Haley's belly hadn't grumbled loud enough to wake the dead. The girl reared her head back and stared at her tummy. "That was loud."

It was completely out of place with what had just happened in their lives, but Tiffany couldn't help herself. She burst out laughing and kept on laughing, until it gave her an excuse to cry.

"Aunt Tiff, you're crying?" Haley's eyes were wide. "But my tummy was funny. And Mama's coming home. Why aren't you happy?"

The child had just summed up everything in a few short sentences, and Tiffany couldn't explain herself if she tried. So, she didn't even try. "I don't know, honey. Maybe I just have to get back to happy after being sad all week."

Haley squinted and twisted her perfect little bow-shaped lips. Then, she nodded. "Okay. What are we going to eat for dinner?"

"Don't know that, either." Tiffany straightened her legs and dumped the child on the floor just before tickling her. "I don't have all the answers. What do you want for dinner?"

"Pizza! With cheese."

"They all come with cheese, bug."

"Just cheese, nothing else. Anything else is yucky." Haley crawled away, and Tiffany let her escape.

For a minute, she allowed herself the luxury of watching Haley's little pale toes with the bright pink nail polish they'd applied on Thursday night clamber across the floor. The agony of letting that go scraped her already-raw throat. "Okay. Cheese for you and weird vegetable pizza for me."

"Weird." Haley had reached the coffee table, where the brand spanking new package of colored pencils distracted her.

Tiffany pushed herself to her feet and exhaled, trying to let all the feelings out. It took only a matter of minutes to order the pizza online—Arch's had her credit card information saved—and then, she stared at her phone.

Shaking spread from her hands to the rest of her, and she grabbed her left arm with her right hand. She was falling apart here. She called Nick before she could change her mind.

"Hey, I didn't expect to hear from you so soon. Something up?" Just hearing his voice made her feel better, and that wasn't good. While he might not be married, there was still the part where he'd left her all those years ago without looking back.

"Yes." She sat on the edge of her desk, the second unlikely place she'd perched in the last hour. She only hoped the furniture and her limbs survived all this. "Emma called. She acted like nothing was wrong."

"What?" He almost growled. Then, he dialed his anger back a notch to a mere snarl. His anger, so much like her own, was the salve her hurting spirit needed. "She just called as if nothing had happened. After putting you and your family through the agony of wondering where she was all week?"

She started to say something—what, she didn't know—because she couldn't defend her sister's actions.

"I'm coming over. Do you want me to pick up something for dinner?"

"What?" Tiffany struggled, but some part of her brain must have functioned. "I ordered pizza for me and Haley. I could order something for you."

Two nights in a row together probably said something, but she wasn't going to worry about the statement.

"Pepperoni on top of pepperoni." He said something to his daughter, and all she could hear was Elloree saying "plain cheese." "Did you hear Elloree's order?"

"Yes." She sniffled. "Same as Haley's."

"Great. Hang in there. I'll be there as soon as I can."

"See you soon." She stared at the phone. At some point, she'd recover enough from this Emma episode to count her blessings again. The fact that she had friends who would drop everything when she needed them would be at the top of the list, after God. Her family might or might not be on there.

She logged on and ordered another pizza.

Then, she walked over and hugged Haley. "Thank you, sweetie, for coloring so nicely while I was on the phone."

"Is Mommy in trouble?" Haley was a smart little girl.

Her promise to never lie had come back to bite her in the butt. "No, sweetie. I'm mad now, but I'll forgive her someday." She bent over and hugged the girl in a mock headlock. "But I do know this—it will turn out all right in the end because God is in charge."

"Yep." Haley tilted her head from side to side like a baby bird. "I'm thirsty now, to go with being hungry."

"Gotcha." Tiffany stood up and stretched. The child's touch and Nick's imminent arrival had brought back a little of her normal sense of self. "The thirsty part I can take care of. The pizza part will have to wait until it gets here."

"Is Ellree coming over?" Haley switched pages. "She's my friend."

Tiffany couldn't believe she was smiling this fast after almost breaking. "Yes, she is. She's coming over, and she's your friend."

"She was funny at church today. I wish I could be funny."

Tiffany would never get the drinks out of the refrigerator if things kept going at this rate. But she'd been taught by some long-ago Sunday school teacher, not her mom, that she should put first things first. And making sure this precious little girl felt good about herself happened to be one of those first things.

Tiffany squeezed into the space between the coffee table and the couch. This was one of those times she was grateful for her small frame. She put an arm around Haley's shoulders and squeezed. "You know, I've always wanted to be funny, too? I've also wanted to be the popular cheerleader, but that was your mama, not me. I wanted to be the brave adventurer, but that was your aunt Shelby. Me, I'm the mouse."

"No, you're not." Haley peered up at her as if she'd grown whiskers.

"Well, I'm not so much anymore, but I used to be really quiet and shy. People didn't notice I was there, and I hid in a corner."

"No, you didn't!" Haley wagged her head back and forth like they were playing a game.

Tiffany realized her niece could protest because she had changed. The mouse wasn't the Aunt Tiffy the little girl knew. She hadn't transformed into a cheerleader and wouldn't be going spelunking anytime soon, but she did stand up for herself, and she had faith in her abilities and God. "I did, but I don't anymore. You don't have to be funny or outgoing or brave if that's not who you are, Haley. Who you are is very special. God doesn't make junk."

"God doesn't make junk." Haley scribbled with a flourish. She might not be funny, but she'd just signed her artwork.

If she didn't know better, Tiffany would say the sleepless and tear-filled nights of this past week had been a figment of her imagination. For a few minutes, she just sat next to her niece and hoped her nearness offered whatever comfort the girl needed.

Haley found another page she liked—this time, one with a princess riding a horse. So, her job done here, Tiffany stood and stumbled over to the kitchen area. It took only a minute to rummage in the refrigerator. "Here's a juice box. I'm going to make some sweet tea."

"I want sweet tea."

"Only when we go out," Tiffany said and then wondered whether this was Emma's rule or her rule. She couldn't remember, and she didn't care what Emma wanted right now. "Wait. If you want sweet tea on the day we found out your mama's coming back, you can have sweet tea."

"Yay!" Haley jumped up and grabbed her aunt in a bear hug. Then, the doorbell rang.

A quick look at the open screen on her computer told her it wasn't the pizza. Tony was only now putting on the toppings.

"Ellree?" Haley yelled through the closed door.

"It's me, Haley. Daddy says we're going to have pizza."

"Yeah, Aunt Tiffany got plain cheese."

The little girls started their chatter even through the barricade of three inches of wood. Tiffany rested a hand on her niece's shoulder and had to force herself not to shake with laughter. "Hey, Haley"—the upheaval of emotions had her voice sounding rusty, as if she hadn't talked in days—"if you back up a few steps, they can come in the apartment."

Haley jumped back. Tiffany huffed out a thick exhale and smoothed her hands over her T-shirt and sweats, which made no sense because she had to look like she'd been run through the wringer anyway. She turned the door handle and did some backing up of her own so she didn't get run over by the hurricane that was Elloree.

"We're here!" The little girl's hair bounced in a high ponytail unlike any Tiffany had seen. It looked like the child had sprouted a unicorn horn.

Haley pointed, not having quite mastered manners. "Your hair's so funny."

Being laughed at didn't faze Elloree whatsoever. She bopped her head like a prancing dancer. "Yep, Daddy did it. He's bad at hair, but that's okay. He's good at being a daddy. Can we go to your room?"

Haley grabbed her friend's hand and pulled her toward the guest room that had really ever held only one guest. The room had pink walls and a white quilt with pink bows tying the block edges. "Aunt Tiffy got me a new doll the other day. Want to see it?"

Their voices faded down the hallway.

Nick's big body filled the doorway. "How are you?"

His voice held so much care and concern that seven years melted away as if they hadn't existed. The hurt that used to be a visceral response when she heard his name got shoved to the side. All she needed to know in that minute was that he had been her best friend for as long as she could remember.

"Um, do you want to come in?"

He crossed the threshold and closed the door gently behind him. He watched her for a few minutes and then held his hands up at his waist, either surrendering or inviting her closer. "Tiff, how are you?"

CHAPTER 16

SHE WALKED RIGHT INTO HIS chest and rested her head. "I'm okay. I feel like I've been beaten up by life, but the bell rang, and the fight's over."

"That doesn't mean you're not still hurting." His arms went around her, but he kept a gap between them. Last night hadn't been pretty, and today had been artificial. They'd been in church, where any kind of real conversation would have been wrong. The attention had rightfully been placed on the girls and the Christmas story.

She allowed herself one more bit of the luxury of human touch. Okay. Not just any human—Nick's touch.

"Can we sit?" He rested his chin on top of her head for a few seconds and then stepped away. "There's a lot to talk about, and the girls are preoccupied for a change."

She nodded, tears perilously close to falling. She felt hollowed out, so maybe this was as good a time as any. They sat on opposite ends of the couch, which didn't put a lot of distance between them given the size of her furniture, but any distance helped.

Before she could find words to say, he held up his left hand. "I took the ring off. I should have done it years ago, but it was sort of final, like saying Lynna never existed."

"You must miss her a lot." She hadn't allowed herself to think about the woman who had been his wife. It was painful enough that she *had* existed.

"Yes and no." He ran his fingers through his hair, causing the curls to stick out in an endearing way. "Don't get me wrong—I loved her, but we weren't best friends like you and I were. We didn't know each other that well—just two lonely marines who found solace together. She was a good marine. I respected her."

"Another hero." Her tone was soft, without any bitterness, because the woman deserved her gratitude.

"Yes, she was." He contemplated her with narrowed eyes. "But so are you, Tiff. I don't even have to walk into your classroom to know you give your heart and soul to educate other people's kids. You don't have to risk your life to be a hero. You just have to give of it."

She turned her body to face him, and her knee almost touched his. That was close enough to reach out and touch him for a heartbeat. "Thank you."

"I meant it. Now, we're left with the bigger questions about why we broke up in the first place. Why you thought I was the kind of man who would pursue another woman while married. I thought you knew me better than that."

"I knew the old you better. I don't really know this you at all."

"If anything, I'd like to think I'm more mature and honorable now than I was back then." He stood and wandered around her small living room, his muscled legs seeming to need the release. "The pizza guy's on his way."

"What?" She'd left the computer screen open. For once, she wanted to push past the distractions. "Oh, by the way, I already paid online."

"Beat me to it, huh?" He gave her a lopsided grin, which said there would be payback at a later date, and that made her happy. "Anyway, let's get back to the reason you called. Tell me about Emma. Where has she been?"

The switch in topics had her dizzy. She wanted to talk about what had happened all those years ago, get her anger out in the open, but now didn't seem the time. She didn't know whether there would be a right time. "Justin's back in her life."

He lifted an eyebrow rather than interrupt her.

"He's Haley's daddy—or birth father, if that's a thing. He went to Lowcountry Tech with Emma, majored in radiology. They were in love, but then, Haley came, and he disappeared."

"And now, he's back." Nick spit out the words as if they left a bad taste in his mouth. "So, how does that prevent her from calling her family?"

"She acted like the first call was enough, but in reality, she didn't want us to know because we don't exactly like him, and then, she was embarrassed that she'd gone to North Carolina without telling anybody. I know it doesn't make much sense." Tiffany rubbed her arms, scrubbing at the chill bumps that seemed to come out of nowhere. "Calling her family. I haven't called anyone, not Mama or Shelby. Oh, dear Lord. Excuse me."

She almost tripped over her own two feet, rushing to grab her phone, but this time, she caught herself.

Her hand was on her phone, and her thumb was sliding over the names. Her mother's contact was a ways down because they hadn't spoken since Monday. That was the relationship they had, the kind of relationship her mother had with all her daughters. They were pretty much cordial strangers at this point.

"Hello?" Her mother's voice creaked, as if she'd aged overnight.

Tiffany swallowed hard at the thought of what her mother must have been going through and the fact she'd extended her pain even for one minute. "Mom, it's Tiffany. I'm so sorry."

"What? Why are you sorry? Is Emma okay?" Her mother's voice got shriller with every word.

"Yes, Mama, she's okay. She's fine. She's just…" Words didn't come.

"Stupid," Nick helped her out.

"Who's that? Who's with you?"

"Nick." Even as she said his name, she realized how surreal all this was. Two of the three sisters were back, to various degrees, with long-lost men. "He moved back to town a few weeks ago."

"He did?" Now, her mother sounded weak. "I have to sit. Why did he say Emma was stupid? Where's she been?"

There was no way to soft-pedal reality. "Emma and Justin are back together, Mom." Her mother groaned, and doubt roiled through her. Maybe this was a story better told in person. "I'm sorry to do this over the phone. I just didn't want to wait any longer."

"What do you mean 'back together'? That boy abandoned her when she needed him the most."

Her mother's questions needed to be answered, regardless of whether this was the best time or place. "Mom, I'm not in a position to defend him or her. But what she told me was that they were just going to North Carolina for the weekend to look at a place to live. The idea was for them to go and be back with no one the wiser. Then, his car broke down, and they were stuck." She had no idea where. Her brain hadn't been fully functioning while her sister told the story. The details would have to wait for another day.

"Anyway, they'll be home on Tuesday when his car is fixed."

Her mother cried on the other end. "She's not dead. My baby's alive."

"Yeah, Mama, she is."

The doorbell buzzed. Nick walked past her with a sly look. She put her hand over the phone, even though she didn't think cell phones worked that way. "Don't you dare."

"Sssh." He winked and pulled out his wallet. "Just taking care of the tip. Talk to your mama."

Her mother said something, and Tiffany walked toward her bedroom. "I'm sorry, Mama. What did you say?"

"I said, y'all think I don't care, but I do. I might not be the best mother in the world, but I kept you clothed and fed when you were kids, and I love all of you."

Tiffany had been doing a good job of holding it together, but now, she shut the door and cried. "I love you, too, Mama."

They didn't have to be perfect. They just had to love each other the best they could.

***

The phone call to Shelby went faster and a whole lot easier, but the others were already eating when she finally emerged. They were squeezed around her small kitchen table and filled the room. Her gaze met Nick's, and it didn't matter that he'd paid when she asked him not to, or maybe it did, and it felt good to be cared for. "Thank you, Nick." She fought a leftover sniffle and, knowing herself, would be doing so for hours. "I really needed that time to talk to my family."

"You're welcome. Glad to be of some help." He gestured to the open pizza boxes on the counter. "I didn't know what you wanted, but I made these greedy little girls save you some cheese just in case."

She glanced at the pizza. There was more cheese left than pepperoni, but his challenge to their character had the girls howling. The veggie pizza was untouched.

"We're not greedy," Elloree said.

"What's *greedy*?" Haley said at the same time.

"Here, Aunt Tiffy," she said, her mouth full. "You sit next to me." She patted the chair between her and Nick.

"So, what's it going to be?" Nick wiped the seat off with a napkin and a flourish. "Cheese, pepperoni, or veggie?"

Tiffany grabbed a plate and one slice of each. "All of the above." She laughed. "I like every kind of pizza there is. And I love sweet tea."

The ice had melted long ago, but even watered-down sweet tea beat every other drink out there. She made her way to the table and sat. Three sets of eyes watched her. "What?"

"We waited to say grace until you came." Elloree dipped her head, and she folded her hands in front of her, fingers squeezed together. "Daddy said we could eat and then ask God to backpack. What did you say, Daddy?"

Nick gave a half grin that lit up one dimple. "I said God can backtrack and bless things in the past, just like he can pre-bless the food. God doesn't live in time."

"And I said I can tell time, so God must know how." Elloree opened one eye and glared.

Tiffany almost choked. "I'm sure He knows how." The golden light in Nick's eyes danced with laughter.

They ate, and the girls filled every minute, and Tiffany started to recover. The girls' innocence, Nick's presence—it all felt unreal. If someone had told her just three weeks ago that she'd be sharing pizza with Nick again after all these years, she'd have accused that person of insanity. She'd been so angry at him for just disappearing from her life. The Nick sitting next to her, the man who'd sneaked to the door and paid for the tip even when she'd already paid, the man who took such good care of his daughter… this man didn't seem like the kind who'd abandon the girl whom he'd promised a future.

The girls were long finished when Nick broke into her train wreck of thoughts. "Penny for your thoughts—or however expensive thoughts are these days."

Tiffany inhaled as if her life depended on it. If she wasn't a mouse anymore, if these last years had meant anything, she needed to find the courage. She twisted in her seat and smiled at Haley. "Hey, Haley bug, why don't you and Elloree go watch a movie? There's not that much time left before bedtime."

The girls scrambled from their chairs and ran over to the living room. The only thing separating the eat-in kitchen was the back of the love seat. Still, the volume would hopefully drown out the adult conversation that was about to take place.

"Wow." Nick grabbed the girls' plates and cleared the table. "I think I need to be standing for whatever this is."

Tiffany took her plate to the sink.

"What do you want to do with the leftovers?" Nick nabbed the last of the pepperoni and wolfed it down so only a few slices of cheese and most of her veggie remained.

"I'll just wrap them in aluminum foil." Tiffany recognized a delaying tactic when she saw one, but she went along since she preferred to procrastinate on this showdown herself. "It makes it easier to bake in the oven. Microwaved pizza isn't worth it."

"Agreed." He opened a random drawer and kept going until he found the right one. Once again, it occurred to Tiffany that he was moving step by step back into her life. First, he'd know where things were in her kitchen, and then, he'd be over for a home-cooked meal. She either needed to nip this in the bud or find a way to deal with the truth.

CHAPTER 17

"TIFFANY, PLEASE, JUST SAY WHAT you've got to say." Nick leaned against a kitchen counter and crossed his arms. The bulge of his biceps beneath the thin dark green sweater distracted her more than it should have.

She tried to meet his eyes but found herself staring somewhere past him instead. "I need to know why you left me all those years ago, why I never heard from you again."

His chiseled jaw set itself in stone. The military-hardened man showed up for the first time since she'd seen him in church. "What are you talking about?" His voice came at her, low and furious. "I wrote you—three times—and you never wrote back. Not once. I was going through the hardest time in my life, and my best friend couldn't bother to drop a postcard."

It hurt to swallow. Her immediate thought was her mother, but her mother had wanted her girls to date. She'd got some strange kind of thrill, as if her daughters' social success reflected on her own attractiveness. She wouldn't have tossed the letters like the evil stepmother in some historical romance novel. "I never received the letters. Why didn't you call?"

He reared back, banging his head against the cabinet. The thud got the girls' attention.

"Daddy, are you all right?" Elloree ran into the kitchen and held out her little hands. "Let me see."

Nick squatted so he was eye level with his little girl and submitted to her clumsy ministrations, which probably made things worse, but, oh, it was enchanting. Elloree patted his head and kissed the top of one of his curls. "I'm sorry you got a booboo. I think you'll be okay."

"Thank you." He pulled her in for a quick hug and rubbed noses. "I'm glad to know."

Elloree skipped back into the living room. "My daddy hurt his head, but he'll be okay," she said to Haley.

"That's good." Haley, who'd been starved for television this last week, never tore her gaze from the all-engrossing screen.

"Don't let my injury fool you. I'm tougher than I look." The man's gaze was impenetrable, his arms back to a barrier. "I couldn't call during basic training. That was the way it works—six weeks of hell, with mail being the only window to the outside world. I looked like a fool, telling the guys when I got there that I had a girl back home, showing them your picture, putting it on the wall next to my bunk. All the stupid soldier things."

Tiffany pushed against her belly with one hand and tried to keep the sick feeling down. "I swear I didn't receive any letters. This sounds stupid, but are you sure you addressed them right? I mean, I don't think my mother would have thrown them away. I don't know." She leaned against the counter for support. "To think, all these years…"

Nick's expression softened to bewilderment rather than accusation. "I'd say call your mother, but I agree. I don't think she would have done that. What about Emma?"

Tiffany tried to remember what had been happening in her life other than the heartbreak of losing Nick. Emma had been a freshman in high school and a brat. "I don't know. That would be a pretty awful thing to do."

"Yes, it would." He gripped the counter now, knuckles standing out with his tight grip. "So, when you didn't write me back, I took it as a sign that you were done. When I could call, I didn't try. Went by the 'three strikes, you're out' rule. What an idiot."

Tiffany's throat was already raw from her tears earlier, but that didn't stop more from coming. "I should have tried. I did call your mother one time and asked how you were doing. She said you were fine, that you'd written her. I thought that if you were contacting her and not me, well, that was all I needed to know."

He took two steps to close the distance between them. "You'd made it clear you didn't want me to go. Do you remember that was the first time we really got into a fight?"

Her heart pounded like that of a cornered rabbit, and speaking of which— "Oh my goodness. I've done it again."

"What?" He leaned forward and placed his hands on the counter, on either side of her body this time. "Stay with me, Tiff. Whatever occurred to you that you need to do can wait. Let's be clear. Neither of us meant for what we had to end. It was all a big misunderstanding."

She looked down and rested her forehead against his chest. "That seems to be the truth. But that was then. That was seven years ago."

He rested his chin on top of her head. They'd done this a lot when they were younger, close but away from those tempting lips and kisses that could have led to where they weren't ready to go. "Are you saying things have changed?"

"No." She breathed against the thin fabric that separated her from his warm skin. "I haven't dated anyone seriously for a couple of years. But are we the same people? Do we still feel the same? You don't just walk back into someone's life and a couple of weeks and—*poof*."

"Poof?" He chuckled and put his arms around her. "You're right. We need time to get to know each other again. I'd like that chance, if you'll give me that chance."

She leaned into his embrace. "I'd like that."

Little hands tugged at their legs, and a little head poked its way into the middle. She'd forgotten about their potential audience.

"Group hug." Haley giggled as she pushed her way between them.

"Haley, when was the last time you had a group hug?" Tiffany's heart constricted, but she kept her voice light and airy.

"When Mommy and my new old daddy hugged at Thanksgiving." The child called Justin "Daddy," and he'd been around at Thanksgiving, and Emma hadn't thought to tell anyone. "He came to my house after we had dinner at Granny Sarah's."

Elloree stood on the outside, looking in. "Can I have a group hug?"

"You bet, princess." Nick stepped back while keeping his arms around Tiffany. His daughter stepped in the middle and twirled, obviously a newbie at this. "Now, you just need to hug both me and Miss Tiffany at the same time."

His instructions caused complete confusion as the two little girls tried to figure out how to hug two grown-up humans at the same time. They all laughed and tried to explain, but Nick never let go. Until finally, Tiffany placed her hands on Elloree's shoulders and turned her sideways before doing the same thing to Haley.

"There we go." They came together in a rush and squeezed.

"I'm being scrunched," Elloree said, but she danced a little jig.

Nick released Tiffany with warmth in his eyes that said the embrace would be continued later. If not that night, other nights. "Time to head home, Elloree. Past bedtime."

"Aaah, do we have to? Can't I stay here?"

"Sleepover, sleepover," Haley chanted, and Elloree joined in.

Nick's dark eyebrows met in the middle. He stared at Tiffany for a minute, and she did her best to remain neutral. She'd welcome the little girl, but it was up to him. After a few seconds, he shook his head. "Not tonight. Miss Tiffany has had a long day and needs some rest. Maybe another day?"

Tiffany startled. "Really, there's only tomorrow night. Your mama's coming home on Tuesday, Haley."

"I could bring her stuff over, if that's okay with you?" He looked wary, as if he was afraid she'd run if he pushed too hard.

Two eager little puppy-dog faces, complete with tongues hanging out and hands begging like paws, tore at her heart. "Oh, all right," she gave in. "We'd love to have you come over tomorrow night, Elloree. I have to warn you, though, that since it's the Christmas season, you might be forced to decorate and eat gingerbread houses."

"Really?" Elloree's eyes widened, and she clasped her hands in front of her. "I've never decorated houses before. Do they taste good?"

Her little nose wrinkled, and the grown-ups tried to stifle laughter. Tiffany leaned over and flipped the ponytail back and forth. "Yes, gingerbread houses are delicious. See you tomorrow about five?"

Nick nudged his daughter toward the living room and their coats. "I'm sorry she invited herself. Is it really okay? That's three nights in a row, and we don't want to overstay our welcome."

"Who's counting?" she said, smiling, even though she knew she was. At the same time, her mixed feelings didn't even want them to leave right now. The thought of the empty apartment she'd be facing for the rest of the holidays, after Emma took Haley back, terrified her. "Really, it's okay. Tuesday, Emma will come get Haley, so this will be my last shot. She'll be taking her to North Carolina." The last was said with such pathos she closed her eyes in embarrassment.

"Hey." Nick tapped her chin. "You'll be fine. We're not going anywhere."

Elloree came bouncing over with her coat buttoned crooked.

"Except home." He bent to fix his little girl's buttons, and Tiffany found herself watching him. They'd lost seven years, and she didn't know whether she wanted to dig any further as to who had done something with his letters and why.

He'd accepted her word at face value that she never received them. She didn't doubt that he mailed them. Earlier, she told Haley that God didn't make junk. Tiffany also thoroughly believed that God didn't make mistakes.

She and Nick might have lost seven years, but he'd gained a beautiful daughter. She'd stuck by her plan to become a teacher, a goal she'd had since third grade, and she had a sneaking suspicion that life as a military wife would have derailed that plan—or at least, slowed it down.

"One snow bunny ready to go." Nick stood, and Tiffany forced herself to move toward the door. It took only a few seconds for him to shrug into his fleece jacket and come to stand in front of her and the open door. "Bye, Tiffany. Thank you for asking the questions that needed to be asked. The old Tiff would have been too scared."

"The old Nick would have gotten defensive and stormed out of here." She met his gaze. Neither of them had been perfect.

He turned a bit redder than the cool air dictated and nodded. "Exactly. Have a good night." He leaned over and gave her a peck on the lips, and she stood there like a deer frozen in headlights.

The girls oohed and aahed.

"Good night," she finally said and stepped back from the door.

"Is Mr. Nick your boyfriend?" Haley had that singsong voice little kids got when they were about to sing the k-i-s-s-i-n-g song.

A distraction was very much needed. Tiffany grabbed her niece and tickled. "You're up past your bedtime, little lady. I think that deserves dire punishment. Dire, indeed."

If Nick wasn't the bad guy, then what was he? Tiffany needed to do more than distract her niece. She needed to distract herself.

CHAPTER 18

MONDAY WAS A WHIRLWIND OF running to the store for gingerbread house—aka graham cracker cabin—supplies and making homemade chicken bog. Tiffany counted on Nick not having changed that much and the dish still being his favorite. Being a single woman with a small appetite, her cooking repertoire was limited. If she'd learned to make her ex-boyfriend's favorite meal years after it was all over and with no hope at the time, well, then, sue her.

When Nick and Elloree showed up promptly at five with a little girl's monogrammed tote bag and flowers in hand, Tiffany melted a little more. It struck her that she might not see Haley as much as she would like after tomorrow, but there would be a motherless little girl in her life in some capacity. After last night's mental wanderings, she forced herself back to the present.

"What is that smell?" Nick didn't even bother with "Hello." He walked into her apartment, still in uniform, and followed his nose. "Tiffany, you didn't. Do you know how long it's been?"

A warm feeling crept into her chest. "Your mother hasn't made it for you? Since you've been home?"

"What is it, Daddy?" Elloree was decked out in a red cape that was much too warm for Charleston but shouted that the child had a meemaw who spoiled her. "What do you smell?"

Nick's eyes danced as he picked up his girl and gave her a little swing. "The best dinner in the world, even though it has a funny name. Chicken bog. Right?" He looked like a little boy promised a bicycle for Christmas.

"Right." Tiffany had been weighed down with her sister returning the next day and Haley leaving. In a few sentences, Nick lightened that load.

She took their coats and started for her bedroom, her normal spot for stashing guests' winter wear, but changed her mind. At some point, Nick would leave, and she felt awkward about having him walk into her room, maybe because he'd been on her mind so much that she'd dreamed about him last night.

Tiffany had the girls help her set the table. Haley showed Elloree where the fork went, and Nick laughed at his daughter's serious face.

"I guess I've always been a little less formal," he said. "What I can cook often involves fingers rather than a knife and fork."

She brought the casserole dish full of seasoned rice, stewed chicken, and sausage to the table. It did something to her insides to have him rub his hands in anticipation. She didn't know whether the way to a man's heart was through his stomach—and why was she thinking of getting to Nick's heart?—but she'd been the one to bring that grin to his face.

"Can I say grace?" Elloree said in her singsong voice. "Please?"

Tiffany wanted to hug her and tell her how proud she was of a child who wanted to say a prayer. She and her sisters had always resisted because of a mixture of mortification and plain old orneriness.

"Of course," Nick said, pride oozing from his whole demeanor. "Thank you, sweetheart."

Elloree glowed. "Can we all bow our heads?" Nothing like following a good role model. They all bowed, but Tiffany and Nick peeked at his adorable child. "Dear God, thank You for this food my daddy says tastes good. Thank You for my new friend, Haley, and her aunt Tiffany. Please, bless our hands and the nourishment of our bodies. Amen."

Tiffany had a grin that really wanted to get out, but she squelched it just in case the little girl would be insulted.

Nick must have felt the same way, though, because he winked at her. "Now, let me at this wonderful meal."

Tiffany passed the crusty French bread around and spooned a small scoop of stew onto Haley's plate. "I cut back on the pepper for the girls. Do you remember that time Grandma overdid it and you were sneezing so hard?"

"I fell out of my chair." Nick served his daughter first and then covered half his plate with the Low Country specialty. "Truth be told, I did it so I could look at your legs. You were wearing these white shorts."

Tiffany glanced at both girls to see whether his words had fazed either of them. They were too busy separating carrots and sausage from the chicken. Deciding it was safe for now, she tried to shoot daggers at the man with her eyes, whatever that meant. "You did not."

His smile was slow and heated. "Woman, you have to remember. I was a teenaged boy, not that different from a twenty-five-year-old man. I would do the same again, given those exact same circumstances."

"Um." Her attraction to the man was returning in leaps and bounds. She had to find a safer subject of conversation. "Do you like the chicken?"

He tilted his head back and laughed.

"What's funny, Daddy?" Elloree had the makings of a counselor when she grew up. "I thought you liked chicken borg."

He hurried and took a bite. It said something—and Tiffany wasn't sure she was ready to explore exactly what—but the man had flirted before digging into his favorite meal.

"It's delicious." Gone was the heated attraction, and in its place was a look of respect Tiffany liked just as much. "Wow, Tiffany, this is good."

"Thank you." She ducked her head and asked him about his day. He'd had a routine day of paperwork and reading lab reports. The science behind detective work reminded her of the television shows she indulged in on nights when she didn't have stacks of grading to do.

"I'm all done." Haley had devoured the chicken, rice, and carrots while her sausage remained untouched. Elloree scrunched up her nose at the carrots but seemed to love the sausage. Between the two of them, they might have a balanced diet.

"So, I guess you're too tired to decorate gingerbread houses?" Nick shook his head, a downtrodden look on his face.

Haley jumped out of her chair and dashed around the room. "Not tired. See?"

"Gingerbread houses, gingerbread houses," Elloree said. She raised the roof with her little hands.

Tiffany was in serious danger of losing her heart to Nick's daughter.

Nick grabbed some plates. "Guess we better clear the table so our overlords can decorate them some gingerbread houses."

"Guess so." Tiffany reached for a glass, but Nick stopped her.

"Why don't you get the ingredients for the houses while I do this?"

She was so unused to help that even this offer seemed a form of romance. "That sounds good. Thank you."

He stacked plates and gave her the full force of his thick eyelashes. "It's the least I can do after you made my favorite dinner."

"Since I usually only cook for my niece, help is unexpected." The graham crackers, gumdrops, and little chocolate candies that were a danger in and of themselves were on a side counter, neatly stacked and ready to go. Sometimes, her first-grade-teacher training came in handy.

By the time Nick had the table cleared and the dishes soaking in the sink, she'd placed paper plates in front of every chair. She stirred a bowl of decorator icing in the middle of the table and spooned some of the glossy sweet stuff into a plastic sandwich bag.

"So, can I decorate, too?" His dark eyes had that puppy-dog begging look. "That is why there's a plate at my chair, right?"

Not all had been sunshine and roses in their earlier relationship. "Only if you promise to be on your best behavior. No cliché icing on my nose or anything resembling a food fight."

He threw his head back and roared with laughter, exposing his lean throat with his later-than-five-o'clock shadow.

She coughed, trying to bring him back to earth. "I'm serious."

"I know you are, and you know me so well." He lifted his chin in defiance. "So, how about this—me and Elloree against you and Haley? Best gingerbread house wins."

She groaned. "Still crazy competitive, I see. But, hey, you're on."

***

In half an hour, they called it quits. Poor Elloree started to tear up when her daddy accidentally knocked over their pitiful little cabin in the last few minutes of competition.

"Don't want to brag, but I think gingerbread mansion beats broken-down shack." Tiffany and Haley did a little victory dance and pulled Elloree up to join hands.

Nick put his head in his hands and winked at her through his fingers. "I'm a beaten man. What I want to know is, where's the mouse I used to know?"

Tiffany stiffened. The girls pulled at her arms. "Dance, Aunt Tiffy. Dance," Haley said.

"She grew up." Tiffany watched for his reaction.

He leaned back in his chair and took a bite of gingerbread doused in icing. "Yes, yes, she did."

They spent the next half hour cleaning up their mess mostly by eating the leftovers. There was the hour of talking around the television more than watching, and then, it was bedtime for the girls, even though Tiffany knew going to sleep would be postponed as long as possible. Nick helped tuck Elloree into the sleeping bag on top of an air mattress, which was the best Tiffany could offer as far as a bed for the little girl. Haley had got jealous and fought to give her friend her bed. Nick solved the argument with a coin toss.

Tiffany kissed her niece's forehead, and pain hit her in the belly. This would be the last time for some time. She wouldn't consider that this little girl, who had started to feel like hers, would be gone.

"Y'all go to sleep for Miss Tiffany, you hear?" Nick exaggerated his accent.

The girls' "Yes, sir" was ruined by their giggles.

Nick held the door, and Tiffany led the way back into the living room.

Nick had his hand on his coat, but he didn't make a move to put it on. "Do you mind if I stay for a little bit?"

"Not at all." Tiffany hugged herself, knowing there was still the barrier of time between them. "Can I get you anything—some coffee?"

They'd had water with their meal, and the dark circles under his eyes made him a really good candidate for some caffeine.

"That would be great." He dropped the coat and followed her into the kitchen. "Can I work on the dishes? I know you said you'd do them, but I'll feel all kinds of guilty if I don't pitch in."

If she was going to let him into her life, even a little bit, she needed to stop treating him like a guest. "Okay, if you insist."

He laughed at a low volume, as if any noise they made would keep the girls awake. "I insist."

She fiddled with her small, garage-sale-find coffee maker, and the silence sat on her back like a pair of stalker's eyes.

"Does this still feel weird to you?" He filled the silence before she could.

She knew exactly what he meant but threw him a confused glance anyway. Last night, she'd been brave. It was his turn.

"I mean, in some ways, it's like I never went away. In others, it's like we're complete strangers."

"Seven years apart will do that to you." She concentrated on not spilling the water. "Maybe we just need time to get to know each other again?"

He rolled up his sleeves, and she tried not to stare at the veins in his forearms. For some reason, she'd always found that level of muscle very attractive. He'd not been this physically fit when he left.

He caught her staring and gave a slow, pleased-with-himself smile. "Time is one thing I have plenty of, Tiffany. Will you let us have that time?"

The good feelings faded. "Why wouldn't I?"

He rinsed a dish, put it in the machine, and rotated to face her. "Do you remember the fight we had, right before I left? I didn't neglect to call you when I got leave just because you didn't reply to my letters. There was a reason to believe that you'd given up on us. Do you remember?"

The chicken bog churned in her stomach. Of course, she remembered. They'd had the fight more than once. "Yes." She leaned against the counter and experienced a sense of déjà vu from the night before. Once again, they were in this same place, talking about hard stuff. "I wasn't comfortable with being a military wife."

When Nick crossed his arms, his shirt bunched, and the police department insignia stood out like a beacon. "You didn't think you could handle worrying about me dying. You were afraid to be alone while I was deployed. You were concerned with traveling to places you'd never been before and not knowing anyone. You were afraid, period."

Tiffany drew a deep breath. "You're not in the military anymore."

He didn't have to say the words; they were so obvious. But he did. "I'm a police detective, Tiff. It's not a whole lot different."

She wanted to yell at him and ask why he needed to put himself in harm's way. Her father had been killed in a robbery. He'd been a security guard at a nearby college. There were good reasons for her fears. "I know."

The coffee percolated behind her, and she went to the refrigerator, her movements stiff. There was hazelnut creamer but no regular half-and-half. If he wanted milk, she had that. When she turned around, he hadn't moved.

"I hoped, after your bravery last night and the way you've welcomed Elloree and me into your life so far, that it wouldn't still be an issue." When she tried to interrupt him, he held up a finger. "Don't get me wrong. No spouse likes the nights of being afraid, and I wouldn't even presume we're that far after a few days of getting to know each other again. It's just that I have Elloree."

She knew that. She'd put frosting on his daughter's nose less than an hour ago.

He touched a wet finger to her nose. "I can't get to know you much better unless I know that you'd at least accept my job. It's part of who I am, Tiff. And I don't want Elloree to fall in love with you if you can't."

Tiffany nodded, knowing he needed a better answer than the bland gesture. "I understand."

She wanted to say more, wanted to be the woman who'd asked the hard questions last night and who'd stood up to her sister, but she might have reached her quota. Seven years of growing was a lot, but underneath, maybe she was the same mouse, after all.

Nick's hands dropped to his sides, and his shoulders gave a little. Her weakness must have communicated itself to him, and he looked older, the shadows under his eyes slashes against his cheekbones. "I'll come and get Ell around nine in the morning, if that's okay with you?"

"Sure." The coffee poured into the pot, each drip echoing like the ticking of an old-fashioned clock. "I'll have her ready."

He lifted his hand toward her and then dropped it. "I'll just finish here and then head out."

Tiffany couldn't stay in the room and know she'd pushed him out of her life—again. "I'll go check on the girls. Good night."

"Good night."

Tiffany's legs ached as if she'd finished a marathon. His reluctance to move forward was right. He had a daughter whose needs trumped their budding relationship, and she understood that. They'd really known each other only for a week this time, early enough to pull out and cause minimal damage.

The only problem was, the damage didn't feel minimal.

CHAPTER 19

NICK CAME AND PICKED UP a very sleepy Elloree at exactly nine o'clock. He gathered the child's things, prompted the child to say thank you, and left. Tiffany had dragged herself through the day like ploughing through pluff mud, and yet, it had sped by too fast. She didn't want to give Haley back to her sister, but the time came regardless of her wishes.

The knock echoed, and Tiffany glanced through the window beside the door. Emma stood outside. Her blond hair was matted to one side of her head, as if she'd slept in the car and then ran to the door without taking time to brush it out. Her eyes were puffy. In other words, her appearance was the complete opposite of the beautiful younger sister Tiffany knew and loved.

Tiffany herself hadn't slept much the night before, what with two giggling little girls who couldn't seem to settle down and her own thoughts yelling at her like a banshee. She was a coward, she was throwing away the best man she'd ever known, and she was stupid. Being kind to the sister who'd put her through agony this past week was going to be harder than normal.

"Tiffany?" Emma sounded like she'd been crying and it wouldn't take much for her to cry again. "Are you there?"

"I'm here, Emma." Tiffany jerked open the front door. "Is Justin with you?"

"No." Emma shrank. Of the three sisters, she was the middle and the tallest. Life didn't always make sense. "We thought it best that I picked up Haley by myself. He wanted to give us some private time, just you and me. And Haley."

Haley was in her bedroom, packing the stuff they'd brought over during the week. Tiffany had wanted her own few minutes with her sister. "Come in, Emma. I shut the bedroom door so Haley wouldn't hear you right away. I just want you to know that I love that little girl, and I love you, but what you did wasn't right."

"I know." Emma looked so young. How was she still young after having been a mother for five years? "I'm so sorry, and I won't ever do anything like that again. I just knew that y'all would be so mad at me for getting back with Justin."

Tiffany hadn't gotten past her anger with her sister to consider the relationship with Justin. Given her confused feelings over Nick, she really didn't have any right to judge her sister. "Oh, Emma, I'm just so glad you're okay." She grabbed her sister and held her. They were both crying when Haley ran into the room.

"Mama. You're here. You're finally here."

She inserted herself in the middle. Group hugs had never been a thing in their family, but the little girl was a fast learner. Emma let Tiffany go and bent to hold her little girl and apologize repeatedly.

Since Emma's phone call on Sunday, Haley had been a chipper little girl, as if her mother's imminent return made everything all right. Her hands grabbing at her mother's shirt, the fingers clawing the fabric as if there were no way her mama was getting out of her sight again, lay waste to that farce. The child had been traumatized.

"I'm going to let Mama know you're here." Tiffany broke into the reunion. She'd learned her lesson about her mother, as well. People didn't have to be perfect to love or to be hurt.

"Do you have to?" Emma said, then squared her shoulders. "Thank you."

Their mother—and Shelby—arrived in fifteen minutes. They must have hit every green light and pushed the speed limit. God had His ways.

Tiffany went into the back bedroom and gathered Haley's stuff. It was amazing how much stuff one little girl could accumulate in less than two weeks. Her fingers almost punctured the stuffed bunny she'd given her niece for Easter, which was now the little girl's wooby. She stared at her hand as if it belonged to someone else. She forced the fingers to relax and said a little prayer for herself, for a change. It was strange how praying about her needs seemed selfish, but right now, she needed some peace in dealing with all this.

"Tiffany," Emma called. "Mama and Shelby are leaving."

Which meant that Emma and Haley wouldn't be far behind. Tiffany lifted her eyes to Heaven, begged for strength to let them go, and pushed herself to move.

"Hey, baby." Her mother gave Tiffany a side hug, all that was possible since Tiffany's arms were full. Her mother already had her jacket on and her big purse swinging.

"Hey, Mama. I'll see you on Sunday for the church potluck?" She tried every once in a while, even though her mother had stopped coming a long time ago. It was strange when the person who'd taught her to worship found other things to do.

Her mother shuffled to the side to let Shelby get her hug in. The older woman concentrated on something in her purse for a minute and then looked up. "Call me and let me know the details."

Tiffany felt a smile coming on. It wasn't a yes, but it also wasn't a no. "I will."

Shelby's blond corkscrew curls bounced when she walked, her athletic build so different from her slender sisters. She grabbed Tiffany in a tight, muscular hug. "Sorry I didn't drop by this week. Work."

Tiffany didn't know what to say. Calling her sister for help hadn't crossed her mind. Their family had fractured at some point, and they needed to find the glue that would get them back together. "It's okay," she lied for now.

Emma followed them to the door and then turned back around. "We need to talk."

Warning bells clanged in the back of Tiffany's mind. "Um, sure?"

Emma closed the door and marched to the couch. "Okay. What is it I heard about the police?"

Tiffany's anger resurfaced as if she were waking from a dream or from a nightmare—up for discussion. "What did you think you heard about the police? You disappeared without letting anyone know where you were; you didn't show up for work. By the way, Jasmine's fired you, you know."

"I would have had to quit anyway," Emma said.

Tiffany had paused only for a breath; she hadn't required an answer. "Most important of all, you left your daughter with me, and as far as I knew, you'd been kidnapped by some guy you met online. That was the only clue I had." Her voice had risen to the point Haley came running back into the room.

The little girl had slipped off into her bedroom, checking to make sure she hadn't left anything behind, the way she'd seen the grown-ups do. "Aunt Tiffy, what's wrong?"

Emma knelt beside her daughter. She brushed back the little girl's bangs. "Aunt Tiffy is mad at me because I did something wrong. She has the right to be angry. Sometimes, it's okay to be mad."

Haley nodded. "As long as you don't do anything bad because you're mad."

The words had come out in a song. Emma rocked back. "Where did you learn that, honey?"

"Church." Haley glanced at Tiffany and grinned. "You're not going to do anything bad, are you?"

Tiffany shook her head, already missing the child. "No, Haley. I'm not. Can you go back into the bedroom and check under your bed? I forgot to look for your stuff there."

"Yes, ma'am." Haley raced off like a rabbit.

Tiffany turned around. Once more, her pet sat on top of her food dish, hungry. She was a terrible pet mother.

"So, you were right to contact the police. I understand that completely. I mean, what do I do now?"

Tiffany reached in her desk drawer for the rabbit food. "I already called, and they closed the case. You might be contacted by Child Services, though."

"Dear Lord." One of the chairs at the kitchen table scraped. Emma sat, her upper body bent over in a shell. "Okay. I deserve that, too. While I sit here and beat myself up, I have to ask. What was Haley saying about Mr. Nick and Elloree?"

Heat flooded Tiffany's cheeks. "What did she say?"

"Don't try to evade the question. Is it your Nick from high school? The one who joined the Marines and never looked back?" Emma crossed her legs, her confidence coming back. "Sounds very familiar."

She was comparing her story to Tiffany's—only, Tiffany hadn't taken off with Nick for another state. Neither had she told her family about his return. She forced herself to finish feeding her bunny and tried to keep the defensiveness out of her voice. "It's not the same." She failed. "Turns out Nick wrote me letters that I never received. He thought I dumped him, and that's a lot better than him knowingly abandoning me and our child, as far as I'm concerned. But it doesn't matter anyway."

Emma's hands flew to her cheeks. "Oh no, oh no."

"What?"

Her sister dropped her head to the table and then met Tiffany's gaze with tears in eyes that should have been bawled dry. "It was me. I can't believe this. You probably don't even remember, but I was really angry with you for telling Mom about me sneaking out at night with Andy. So, I hid your letters. I'm so sorry."

Disbelief washed over Tiffany's skin, and then turned to red-hot fury. She pivoted and walked out of the apartment. The chilly December air took a little while to cool her down. All these years, she could have been with Nick. They'd lost seven years—and all because of some petty revenge on the part of her teenage sister.

Well, now, they had their answer. Tiffany rubbed at arms covered with chill bumps and sighed. All those years, and there was no way to go backward, no way to get them back. She reached the stop sign at the end of her street before turning around. She passed her next-door neighbors and forced herself to nod, to act as if everything were okay. At the door, she concentrated on calming her heart rate to a less murderous pace before turning the handle.

Emma sat at her miniscule kitchen table with tears running down her face. When Tiffany crossed the room, her sister held out an upturned hand and mutely begged for forgiveness.

Tiffany couldn't find words, but she prayed for strength. God had His ways. Still, she moved to the couch rather than touch her sister yet. "I'll work on forgiving you. It may take some time. Besides, like I said, it doesn't really matter in the long run."

"Why?"

"Nick and I aren't meant to be." The words sounded harsh—and weak—as they left her mouth.

"Why?"

Tiffany shivered even as the heat poured out of the vent above her head. Emma was planning on quitting two jobs and moving to another state to be with a man in the military. "Because he's a police officer."

Emma came to sit right next to her, with nothing between them but a throw pillow. "Are you telling me you're going to give up the love of your life, for the second time, because of fear? Aren't you the only one of us who's stuck it out at church? Where's that faith now?"

Tiffany might have been a mouse all her life, but she'd never run out of words before.

Emma reached over and placed a hand on Tiffany's, where she had them clasped on her lap. Emma was wearing an engagement ring. Tiffany lost her breath.

"Mommy, can we go home? I'm sleepy."

Would wonders ever cease?

CHAPTER 20

TIFFANY BRUSHED HER HAIR ONE last time and outlined her lips with pale pink lipstick. She contemplated the contents of her jewelry box that had nothing in it worth over twenty dollars, except her class ring, and riffled through the few gold chains. An index card poked out. Her first year of teaching, one of the mothers had given her a silver cross on a chain and this lined index card with a thank-you note.

Thank you for a wonderful semester. Emily loves your class and is learning so much. Proverbs 3:5. Mrs. Connell.

For some reason, Tiffany had stuffed the card in the porcelain box, along with the necklace. Now, the Bible verse challenged her like a riddle. She had to know what it said. She'd never been good about memorizing verses, but her well-worn Bible lingered on her nightstand.

"Trust in the Lord with all your heart and lean not on your own understanding."

She flicked another glance upward just as the doorbell rang. Nick, this time alone.

Tuesday, Emma had taken Haley home. Tiffany had binge-watched old movies and eaten enough popcorn to dry her lips out with salt. Wednesday, Tiffany and Haley had met Nick and Elloree on Summer Creek's Main Street. They'd walked around the Christmas tree displays and had lunch and bubble tea at the Soup and Saucer, a sandwich shop on the corner.

She and Nick had acted like nothing was wrong. They laughed with the girls, inquired about each other's days, and kept everything at a surface level.

Then, when he walked her and Haley back to her car, Nick dropped all pretensions. "Tiffany, can we get together Friday night? I know it's the day before Christmas Eve, but I'd like to see you, just you and me."

She hesitated. There was a point at which they were just torturing themselves.

"It's just one date, Tiffany." He rushed in before she could say no. "Give you a taste of what you'll be missing." His wink started the girls giggling.

She already knew what she'd be missing, but she also couldn't break it off completely, not yet. Not after Emma's challenge. So, she said yes. Now, she wanted to smack herself for being a pushover and check her makeup one more time—both simultaneously.

The doorbell rang. He'd gone from knocking to ringing, and she was still in her bathroom. She gave the woman in the mirror a mean look and told her to be strong. She swung open the door as the bell chimed one more time. "Sorry. I had trouble figuring out what to wear."

He wore jeans and a dark green pullover. She'd finally settled on a sweater dress. One of them wasn't dressed for the occasion. Since they'd never gotten past the day and time, she had no idea what he had planned.

"Hi." He gave her a crooked grin, and she found herself smiling back, despite all the misgivings. His curls looked slightly damp. He'd rushed home and showered, and his hair hadn't completely dried. He held out a box and an envelope. "I could bring you flowers again, but I know you're a food kind of girl instead. I bought this yesterday."

"Would you like to come in for a minute?" She took the plain white box, but he held on to the envelope. She stood to the side.

He walked by, his shoulders filling the doorframe and then his presence filling the room. She glanced inside the box to give her heart a break, except it only made that part of her ache more. "Red velvet. You remembered."

Nick hadn't gone far; only a few feet separated them. "Told you I was going to give you a taste of what you'd be missing."

She gave him as big a grin as she could manage. "Literally?"

"Yes, literally." He laughed. "So, to continue our trip down memory lane, I thought we'd go to the mall and eat at the food court."

She gave him a sideways glance. "Really?"

His smile evaporated, leaving a neutral face she couldn't see through. He took the box from her and walked into the kitchen. He placed the envelope on the counter and the cake in the fridge and then shoved his hands in his pockets. "No, not really. I have reservations at The Plantation on Isle of Palms. But I don't know if I can do this."

For the first time, she saw the hint of dark circles under his eyes. He was too young for deep laugh lines, but exhaustion showed at the corners of his lips and in the set of his back.

"Do what?" she asked, even though it was an inane question. She was stalling, recognizing it in herself, but she couldn't stop herself, either.

"This." He waved his hands between them. "I didn't plan on asking you out. I was going to let you go, but then, you were walking toward your car, and I saw myself in your position seven years ago. There was no way I was going to stand there and watch you drive out of my life." He ran his hand through his hair and tilted his head. The pain in those dark eyes had no limit. "So, I started thinking about what I could do with my life if I wasn't a cop. I could teach at the academy or maybe criminal justice at the technical college, if that's what it takes. Tiff, I can't lose you again."

It was a good thing he'd relieved her of the cake, because she would have dropped the box. The loss of her favorite dessert would have made her sad, but what Nick proposed would be a tragedy.

"No," she whispered. "That wouldn't be right. My fear has prevented me from so much. I can't let it keep you from being who you were meant to be. And you were meant to protect people. You were meant to be a hero."

With every word she'd said, she'd taken a step. The old Tiffany had done a lot of running away. The new Tiffany touched Nick first and rested a hand on his cheek. He'd done nothing but track her progress and wait. "I decided that I'd rather live with you and trust in God than live without you."

He turned his head and kissed her palm. "What changed?"

She gave a one-shoulder shrug. "God—and Emma—talked some sense into me."

Her hand now rested in his, and he interlaced their fingers. "God and Emma? I don't know which is harder to believe."

One last step, and she leaned against his chest, always one of her favorite places to visit in the world. "Emma is taking a chance on Justin, and he's still in the military. And on Tuesday, she pointed out that I was the sister who was supposed to have faith."

"And God?" His arms came around her.

"I was actually late because I found a thank-you note from a student's mother in my jewelry box. Don't ask me why it was there." She leaned back to look him in the eye and liked the glimmer she saw there. "There was a Bible verse at the bottom—or the reference to one, at least. I looked it up."

"And?" He kissed her cheekbone.

"'Trust in the LORD with all your heart.'" Remembering the words would have been difficult even if she'd memorized the verse, since a gorgeous man was kissing the tip of her nose and the words flew out of her head. "And something more. If I trust in Him, I'm not supposed to fear, right?"

"I don't take any chances if I can help it. There's more paperwork than you can imagine, and this is Summer Creek, South Carolina, one of the safer places in the world." He kissed a trail leading to her lips. "I have a daughter who means the world to me. My mother. And you."

He reached the end of the trail, and this kiss wasn't a peck in front of nosy little girls. This was a kiss seven years in the making and a promise of many more years to come. Tiffany grabbed his broad shoulders and gave herself to the kiss. Her body started to respond, and she broke the embrace.

"What time were those reservations?"

He stepped sideways and made a show of reading the magnets on the front of her refrigerator. A quick glance at his watch, and he smiled a crooked smile, without the shadow he'd walked into her apartment carrying. "We still have time. Get your coat?"

"I'll be right back." Tiffany rushed toward her bedroom.

When she came out, he was nowhere to be found. A noise in the bathroom let her know he hadn't decided to make a run for it. She dropped the coat on a chair and wandered. Bunny Foo Foo nosed his way to the edge of the cage, and she buried her fingers in his fluffy black-and-white fur. For once, she'd fed him earlier in the morning. Waiting any later in the day had proven dangerous.

The envelope Nick had brought with him beckoned on the counter like a love note someone passed in class to pass to someone else. The temptation to at least peek expanded. It was a book-sized envelope, and he'd scrawled her name in block print across the front.

"I might not have called, but I never stopped thinking about you." Nick came down the hallway. "Open it."

She rubbed her arms to ward off the goose bumps that came out of nowhere. She flipped the envelope over and ran her finger under the tape. The paper had a yellowed sheen of time and hard use. Inside were ticket stubs and postcards from places around the world. "Wish you were here. You'd hate it; it's too hot, and there's no sweet tea, but still wish you were here."

"Don't cry." Nick must have seen it coming before she did.

Tears pooled at the corner of her eyes. "How could I not?"

"I know." He waved an object in front of his face. He was still across the room. The contents of the envelope broke some wall inside her, and all she wanted was to be held. She turned and started toward him. She tripped over her own two feet.

This time, he caught her, and she welcomed the rescue. Being strong didn't preclude accepting a hero rescuing her when she needed one.

"Hey." He laughed. "I didn't mean to make you upset. Listen. I found something that'll make you laugh."

"What?" She found her island swimsuit Santa staring her in the face. "Oh no."

"No? You don't like Santa?" He rubbed her nose with his. Old Saint Nick started singing, unprompted. "Oh, wow, that's awful."

He shoved the ornament down between the couch cushions, where only a muted verse about an island paradise could be heard. His gaze landed on the miniature Christmas tree a few feet away.

Tiffany blocked his path. "Oh, no, you don't."

He gave her a slow grin that spread to his glittering eyes. "Did you keep it?" His feint to one side was a move she expected, but she couldn't stop him when he lifted her and moved her out of his way. "I can't believe it. You kept it. Where is it?"

She made one more attempt to prevent disaster. He'd just come back into her life. "It's hidden where you'll never find it."

Nick grabbed the one ornament facing the wall. "Aw, you put it where no one could see it. Tiffany, the memories."

The cheap photo ornament, in a simple frame that he'd bought at a kiosk in the center of the mall, contained pictures of them in all their high school glory. He was full brace face, and her straggling hair accentuated features not quite ready for prime time. She'd been so thin and her eyes so large. Friends—or maybe they hadn't been friends—had called her "the hobbit."

"It's awful."

"You kept it." He exchanged the blackmail-worthy ornament with a spun-glass manger scene smack dab in the middle. "That was the first time we hung out, as friends, and we went to see Santa like the couple of kids we were."

She leaned against him and stared at her tree. "Then, we got there, and Santa was done for the day, so we went to the photo booth and took those silly pictures."

"First picture. First date. You were beautiful."

She stared at him over glasses, which she wasn't wearing because she never wore them around him. "It's best not to start your fresh start by lying."

He kissed the top of her head. "I'm not lying. Look at those eyes, so innocent and sweet, the kind of person who would keep this ornament all these years. I know we just began our fresh start, but, Tiffany Marano, I love you."

Her eyes closed, and she leaned against the wool of his coat and his strength. "I love you, too." Her stomach growled, loud enough to drown out Santa. "Now, feed me, man."

"It's always food with you, woman."

He drew her back against him for one more kiss, but she slipped away. She laughed and headed toward the door. "Yep. Food and Christmas and Jesus and Haley and Elloree."

She glanced back. "And you."

EPILOGUE

Two years later…

"I GET TO SEE HIM first."

"No, me. He's my cousin." Haley elbowed her friend out of the way. Her mother groaned behind her.

Elloree threw her own pointed elbow. "He's my brother. Brothers are more importanter than cousins."

Nick's arm snaked around his firstborn and lifted her up and away from the hospital bed. "You're both important, and Jacob will love you both. But you can't see the baby unless you behave. Say you're sorry to your friend."

"She's not my friend. She's my cousin," Elloree argued.

"Good grief." Emma wrapped her arms around Haley's neck in a loose hug. "Is there such a thing as sassy six? It may be worse than the terrible twos."

"I'm thinking that every age has its challenges." Tiffany spoke for the first time since welcoming her family into the room. It was the first time she'd gone through labor, but she'd been a mother for a year. Her voice was hoarse, and every part of her body hurt, except maybe the arm cradling her son. "Elloree, say you're sorry so you can see your new brother. His eyes won't be open long."

"Sorry," Elloree whispered, and they took what they could get. Nick had a ten-o'clock shadow, his dark eyes had darker shadows, and he'd never looked more handsome. He positioned Elloree with her feet on the bed rail so she could peer into the bundle that was their squinty-eyed, red-faced Jacob.

"Be gentle," Nick said in a hushed voice, reverent. He'd been with her every minute of this labor, the terror still in the corner of his eyes. He'd not said it, not while the doctors and nurses did their job, reassuring them with every word that mother and baby were doing fine, but his real fear had been there in the way he searched her eyes. When he thought she wasn't looking, he'd kept his silent vigil, watching for any sign. He'd been worried sick that he'd lose her.

"I thought you said he was beautiful." Elloree snorted. "He's all wrinkly and red in the face. He's—"

Nick put a hand over the girl's mouth. "He's beautiful because we love him, not because of how he looks. He's healthy, and your mama's healthy, and that's all that matters."

Elloree rose up on her tiptoes. She twisted and caught her daddy's face between her hands. "You sound funny. Daddy, are you crying again? Mama seems to make you cry a lot."

"No, she doesn't." Nick smiled at Tiffany around his daughter's mass of hair. "She makes me happy a lot."

"I love you, Nick." Tiffany repeated what he'd really said.

"My turn!" Haley escaped her mother's arm circle.

Emma made a half-hearted attempt to stop her daughter but ended up helping her into place next to Elloree. Tiffany smiled at her sister and did her best to stifle a yawn.

Jacob yawned back, in complete agreement with his mother.

"He's tired." Haley dared to touch his cheek with a finger, and the baby rooted in her direction, mouth sucking like a goldfish. "And he's hungry. You need to feed him, Aunt Tiffy."

Justin coughed. "Well, that's our cue. He's beautiful, guys. Congratulations."

Tiffany smiled, but she didn't think she could speak without yawning in everyone's face again.

"Thank you, man. He's looking forward to meeting his cousin." Nick nodded with his chin in the direction of Emma's bulging belly.

"Yeah, we can't wait to meet him, too." Emma rested her hand on top of what looked to be a protruding foot, and Justin kissed her cheek.

"Good night," Shelby said from where she hovered near the door. The only remaining single among them, she'd been on the outskirts looking in this last year of weddings and baby showers and couple everythings. "I'll come by your house tomorrow night, if that's okay, Tiff? I have something to give you."

Tiffany almost asked what it was, but the guarded expression in her sister's eyes stopped the question. Shelby always had her reasons. She'd been their father's little tomboy and had taken his loss the hardest, if that was possible. Since then, even before the onslaught of men in their lives, she'd always reserved some part of herself, away from them. "I'll look forward to seeing you. Love you, Shels."

"Love you. Congratulations, Nick." She backed out the door, as if she couldn't escape fast enough. "See you, Emma, Justin."

The furrow in Emma's brow smoothed when she turned back toward the bed. "Good night, Tiff. Love you guys."

Haley jumped down from the bed, almost going too far and leaping into Justin's arms. "Good night, baby Jacob. Come on, Elloree. We're having another sleepover at your house."

Elloree planted a smooch on her now-sleeping brother's cheek. "Good night, brother. Good night, Mom. Good night, Dad. Bye."

Nick's mouth twisted in a mock scowl as his daughter skipped off into the sunset without a backward glance. "Well, good to know we'll be missed."

They watched the room empty. Her mother had been there earlier and had Jim drive her home before it got too dark to see.

Tiffany reached out the hand not holding a warm bundle of joy, and Nick grabbed it. He leaned over the bed and inhaled, rough edges to his breathing. "I have to pray, Tiffany. Right here and now."

"Yes, please."

"Father God, thank You so much for keeping Tiffany and little Jacob safe." Nick's voice was low and urgent. "I don't know what I'd have done." His swallow was audible. "So, anyway, thank You more than I can say."

"Amen," Tiffany said as his hand convulsed in hers. "Hey, Nick, I'm right here, not going anywhere."

"I know." He kissed her forehead and then again, as if to put a period on his worry. "Hey, do you know what time it is?"

She blinked at the abrupt change of topic, confused, and to fight off impending sleep. "No. Why?"

"It's after midnight." He kissed her again, and she leaned into his touch. "On Christmas."

A sense of lightness filled her. "A Christmas baby."

"I can't think of a better gift."

She couldn't, either. She didn't protest when he extricated the baby from her grip, because for a moment—maybe more—everything in her world was right where it belonged.

ABOUT THE AUTHOR

A member of American Christian Fiction Writers, Christina Sinisi writes stories about families, both the broken and blessed. Her works include a semi-finalist in the Amazon Breakthrough Novel Award contest, and finalists in a number of writing contests, such as the American Title IV Contest where she appeared in the top ten in the Romantic Times magazine. By day, she is a psychology professor and lives in the LowCountry of South Carolina with her husband and two children and loves a good cooking challenge. Please visit her at Christina Sinisi-Author on Facebook and christinasinisi.com.

www.ChristinaSinisi.com

Made in United States
Orlando, FL
16 March 2024